# The Secrets of the Camera Obscura

# *The Secrets of the Camera Obscura*

NOVELLA BY DAVID KNOWLES

CHRONICLE BOOKS
SAN FRANCISCO

Printed in the United States of America

Library of Congress Cataloging-in-Publication Data:
Knowles, David, 1966–
The secrets of the camera obscura / David Knowles.
p. cm.
ISBN 0-8118-0655-3
1. Camera obscura—Fiction. 2. Murder—Fiction. I. Title.
PS3561.N677S43 1994
813'.54—dc20 93-30339
CIP

Book and cover design: Gretchen Scoble
Composition: On Line Typography
Cover photograph: Thea Schrack

Distributed in Canada by Raincoast Books,
112 East Third Avenue, Vancouver, B.C. V5T 1C8

10 9 8 7 6 5 4 3 2 1

Chronicle Books
275 Fifth Street
San Francisco, CA 94103

*Many thanks to*
*Owen Phillips*

# CAMERA LUCIDA

BEFORE THE MURDER I would sit alone for close to four hours inside the camera obscura, writing. Cloudy days, when visibility drops to just a few feet, I flip the CLOSED sign, brew a fresh pot of coffee and lock the doors. The fog rolls in from the ocean and the camera screen goes gray. Steam rises from my coffee and mingles with the fog's marbleized patterns, in a slow, hypnotic dance. After five minutes or so of staring into the screen I'd begin writing. Through the winter months I could fill five, maybe six blue notebooks, the small-lined notebooks.

Of course, the stories always involved the giant camera. I have compiled what is perhaps the world's most detailed record of the camera obscura, starting with the Chinese inventors and continuing right up to the present day, and it is the *kind* of detail that separates my writing from other studies, from *A Chronicle of the Camera Obscura,* by John Hammond, or *The Camera in Art and Science,* by Simon Shiller.

While those books do provide an excellent overview, they unfortunately gloss over and even ignore key portions of history. In my journal, however, I recreated each and every setting. I'd see it all on the camera's screen in stunning clarity. In those moments of solitary meditation and reverie I became the conduit for history, the recorder of events that, without my testimony, would have slipped away from the world unnoticed.

Mind you, it wasn't always this way. In fact, the life of the journal is fairly new to me. Three years ago my writing was unfocused and infrequent. Journal would have been the wrong word altogether. Better put, a scrap book to store phone numbers, newspaper clippings, dates in history, etc. Slowly it progressed into a daily log of events and personal impressions of those events. What the customers looked like, if they said anything unusual. At the end of the day I would conclude my entries with long aesthetic reflections on the camera obscura itself, on the beauty of its images.

As time passed my writing grew more lucid until I reached a point where I could go for hours without knowing what in particular I was writing about, a kind of random, automatic pilot. Finally I began to focus on the behind-the-scenes history of the camera, and the evolution was complete. At present the journal takes up several notebooks, volumes if you will, that I stack together underneath my cramped desk in the ticket booth. Well over two-thirds of the books explore the history of the camera obscura.

It wasn't until the murder of the woman from Florence, however, that I began to focus on the patterns in the journal. Recurring historical circumstances within the writing involving the Chinese, Italians, and the Dutch. Before the day they found her on the cliffs, I would have said that the stories didn't have much to do with me, other than the simple fact that I took the time to write them.

According to the newspaper article the murder fit the description of a series of similar crimes involving missing body parts. Crimes of this sort, the newspaper claims, always seem to travel in groups. The newspaper is right, much more so than they could have known, and the evidence lies within the pages of history. Because of her I've started trying to make sense of all the old stories and journal entries, studying them for clues.

Her body was discovered by a tourist at Lookout Point nearly one month ago, lifeless on the concrete path, decapitated, only a few hundred yards from the camera. What's even more disturbing is the fact that I saw her on the cliffs the day she died. Only hours, as it turns out, before the crime took place. I watched her through the camera obscura. Surely you can see how I feel personally a part of the whole thing.

# DARK CHAMBER

I SHOULD EXPLAIN the camera obscura now before I go much further. If you're going to understand the stories that follow then you've got to have a clear working picture of the machine. Looking at the building you'd never guess what lay inside. The cold, beige painted concrete and the box-like architecture suggest little more than a storage shed or utility space. The only clues are the black letters, GIANT CAMERA, painted on the east wall.

In those words lies the key to understanding the machine, for when you pass into the small dark chamber you have entered the insides of a camera, a camera in which you are the film, or more precisely, your memory is. It takes your eyes a few minutes to adjust to the dim light. Thick black velvet lines the walls and ceiling, and the floor is coated with black paint. The doors seal tightly so that darkness is maintained. In the center of the room rests a circular screen, three and a half feet in diameter, which acts as the focal point for light that enters the chamber from a kind of periscope in the ceiling. The whole thing is done with mirrors. What you get is the live image of the outside world, the cliffs to the north, the ocean, the windmills in the park, or the long beach and coastline to the south, displayed in front of you on the screen. Best of all, the periscope rotates, one complete circle every six minutes, so that the pictures revolve around the screen to provide a full panorama of the stunning seascape. The difficult part comes in describing the emotions which gazing down at the screen evokes. I'm not sure one could adequately write down this phenomenon. Really, it falls under the category of *you have got to see it for yourself.*

I can tell you a story to put things in perspective. One spring day a few years back an elderly lady happened to visit the camera. She had never heard of the camera obscura and asked me if it was the kind of show an old woman like herself would appreciate. Why of course, I said, the show is as timeless, as blind to age, as they come. A show for all ages! She gladly purchased a ticket and entered the chamber.

Well, not more that two minutes pass before she walks right out again and asks me, "How long before the show starts?"

And I say, "This *is* the show." To which she just looks very confused.

"Well don't you have any other films to play? I mean this one's a bit on the boring side if you want my honest opinion.

Sure it's pretty to look at, but where's the story?" So I lead the woman back into the camera and try to explain that what she's watching isn't a movie or a video, but the outside world as it is passing at that precise moment. But here's the thing, she absolutely refuses to believe me, in fact she just starts laughing out loud. "The real world looks nothing like this," she says. "Now please put on another selection." I left it at that, partly because I believed her. The camera *does* portray the world in a much more beautiful light than the naked eye alone.

This encounter made me flash back to what I had read about the audience's response to the first motion picture. In the film, a steam locomotive headed straight for the camera, giving the viewer the uneasy sensation that the train would surely crash directly into the camera and hence through the screen itself, crushing the audience in a matter of seconds. As the train sped toward the imagined boundary of the screen nearly half of the people jumped out of their seats and ran screaming for the exits. They fully believed that the train would barrel over them, slaughtering an entire theater of innocent victims. Their trust in the images was total. Conversely, however, the old woman mistrusted her eyes so much that she couldn't recognize the real world as it looked up at her.

While the images one gazes upon are in fact actually happening only a few feet away, the experience of looking at the camera screen evokes feelings of solemnity and awe, though perhaps not for the old woman, perhaps not for those who don't appreciate subtlety. Floating is what it feels like to me, or that I'm inside of a submarine, probably because of the periscope. Take the sensation of looking through a normal-sized camera, of pointing and capturing a single frame, now multiply that feeling a hundred times over, a thousand times, who could say how many times? Perhaps it's immeasurable. It's best just to remember *Giant Camera.* I am the owner of the giant camera, and I work in the ticket booth seven days a week.

I lead a simple life, not filled with extravagances or frills. Routine dictates my existence. Finding me isn't hard. You've really got only three options: the camera obscura, the main branch of the public library, or my apartment out on Thirty-seventh Avenue, located only blocks from the beach and the camera. Also there's my car. Four places if you count my car, which I drive from my house to the camera in the morning, from the camera to the library in the evening and from the library back to my apartment when the library closes at seven-thirty.

I inherited my car, a navy Plymouth Valiant, from my father along with the camera obscura when he drowned one summer while swimming out in front of the cliffs. Rip tides take a few people each year, but my father considered himself too good a swimmer to ever drown. I was twenty-nine years old, and quit my job as a book store clerk to run the camera. At the time I knew relatively little about the machine but figured that anything had to be better than stocking books eight hours a day. My father never talked to me about the camera, and what I know of it today I learned on my own. I live alone in this world, save the visits from a few regular customers, and the journal has become my one enduring passion.

# THE HANDS OF TIME

THE ITALIAN WOMAN often visited the camera so we had occasion to exchange words now and then. In fact I believe that it's not unreasonable to think that she considered me a friend.

"Hello again," I say.

"Hello. How is business?" Her usual reply.

"Fine. Fine considering all the rain."

"Not a problem today," she says.

"No, clear as a bell." And then an awkward silence. "You should come in for a sunset one of these days," I offer.

"Maybe I will," she says entering the chamber. We had dozens of similar, incidental conversations.

What I know for sure is that she was a woman in trouble, running from a horrible life back in Italy. Men, she said. Mainly she ran away from the men in her life, all of whom were either painters or photographers. Men who she modeled for. It's not hard to imagine why she left, is it? I've known men to act like beasts for a lot less. Could the murderer have been one of those wretched Italians? One who tracked her down, across an ocean and a continent? Perhaps, though she made her relationships back home seem less dangerous, lecherous yes, but not life-threatening.

What my camera obscura was for her is hard to say. An oasis? An escape? She would remain inside for hours, staring at the circular screen, which is precisely why I first noticed her. You could protest and say that her beauty first got me hooked, but really I swear it was her obsession with the camera that made me curious. Few people stay inside for so long. In fact most just don't get it. They can see the camera's beautiful images right in front of their own eyes, they can even acknowledge the beauty, but hardly ever do they *appreciate* it. After the third or fourth visit I stopped charging her altogether.

There were times when my mind would stray, fantasize. She'd be inside the camera, lost in the images on the screen. Usually I approached her from behind, my shoes not making a sound. Slowly I slide my hands across her waist, down her flat stomach. I'm not embarrassed to admit such things. Faithfully, I wrote down detailed accounts of these fantasies each time they would come to me. Eventually they began to take up large sections of the journal.

Old world beauty is what I would call it. Black hair, shoulder length. About five-six, which is a perfect compliment to my five-eight. Thin but with healthy curves. Bright eyes, radiant, so radiant that they didn't look real. A tight-lipped, understated smile that drove me wild with its coyness.

I often wrote about the woman, though I never told her. I'd try to imagine her life back in Italy, or use her as the main character in a love story. Stories set in the time of Leonardo da Vinci. Usually she would have a double identity, on occasion triple. A spy, thief, model, foreign dignitary. But most of all I'd write the story of the two of us together inside the camera. I promised myself that I wouldn't ever show anyone that story. What I wouldn't do to turn back the hands of time. To have another chance with her.

In the journal I can trace the moment that I fell in love with her. The entry begins, "Sun, after a week of rain ..."

## NOTEBOOK 8, PAGE 37

SUN, AFTER A week of rain, sun. A crisp horizon out to sea. Today a real development occurs. She comes in a bit early, 11 a.m., usually it's 1 or 2 during her lunch break. This makes me a bit nervous, perhaps because I hadn't prepared myself for the possibility of seeing her. She smiles, as usual. "Hello there," I say.

"Hello," she replies.

"How's everything?"

"Fine." Obviously she's not in the mood to talk.

"Well, enjoy the show." I wave her inside, and she enters the chamber.

In the ticket booth I find myself in the now chronic position, turned around staring at the print of the Mona Lisa that hangs behind me. Go inside, I tell myself, do it. I never know what the Mona Lisa thinks. Is she mocking me? She must be. But what for? Most of the time when I look at her face, her smile soothes me, puts me at ease, like she's telling me everything's all right. But occasionally, like today, she looks at me with what feels like pure contempt, pure mockery. Some days I can understand the look, say I tell a bad joke, or lock myself out of the ticket booth. Though today I can't honestly say what the reason would be. What does she expect? That I barge in on the woman from Florence again, like I've done so many times in the past? To show her how to control the periscope, or to check for another leak in the ceiling? No, no, no! The last time, when I said I had been hearing complaints about a mysterious draft, the look on her face told me that the excuses had worn thin. Sure she smiled and nodded, but I could read tension all over her face. The smile was fixed into place and had no connection whatsoever to anything I had said or would say, it was courtesy. I immediately recognized the look and rushed out of the chamber with a kind of humiliated shuffle.

Deep down I know in my heart of hearts that Mona accepts me with all of my faults. Not that falling in love with a beautiful woman could be considered a fault! Surely the Mona Lisa would never assert such a claim, considering how many men fell head over heels for her in her time. Perhaps I misread her smile, the Mona Lisa's I mean.

Twenty minutes go by. I reach for the pack of emergency cigarettes I keep behind the stack of notebooks underneath the desk, when suddenly, incredibly, unthinkably, there's a knock at the door. The door which leads from the ticket booth to the chamber. It goes without saying that I freeze, that I'm sure I've just imagined the knock to trick myself into opening the door. But sure enough another knock sounds, then a louder, quicker knocking. I'm sweating and I know I'm sweating. I stand up, walk to the door and turn the handle. She stands with her hands at her sides, perfectly framed by the doorway, squinting at first from the sunlight. She says, "I'm sorry to disturb you, but can you tell me how it works?" All in the accent. Slowly her eyes begin to relax.

I can't tell you what I was thinking at that moment. Thinking certainly didn't factor in much. Reacting would be a better word, but what I do remember are her eyes, those green, magnificent eyes.

How it works? How it works! After all the hours she stood inside watching the screen, the endless repetition of the fifteen-minute audio cassette explaining in painful detail the history and operational mechanisms. I think about it mathematically for a moment, three times a day for over two months. After all of this she still doesn't know how the beautiful image appears. She understands and speaks English fluently. Could it be true that until this moment none of that mattered even one little bit? That beauty was beauty for whatever reason. Or was she just looking for an excuse to talk to me? Or perhaps both possibilities were true. It was then, looking down at her while she awaited my response, her eyes penetrating my soul, that I realized I loved her.

"Mirrors," I say.

## JANUARY, AT LAST

I HAVE ONCE again endured the summer, the fall, and finally the holiday season. This year the admission receipts totaled a new high, perhaps because of the murder, a sickening thought. Gawkers came in large numbers the week after the newspaper story to get a glimpse at the exact spot she was killed. The public's macabre fascination never ceases to amaze me. Old ladies, whole families even! They'd sit in the camera, fairly silent until the periscope rotated around and pointed towards the cliffs, focusing on the taped-off portion of the path, then it was all hysterical banter. "How did she die?" "Murdered!" "The killer is on the loose!" "Do you think he'll strike again?" "How awful! How truly awful this world is!"

The normal cycle of business extends eight months, April through December, a time when my mind focuses on making enough money to keep the camera open in the slow months. I turn into a salesman, barking out my pitch to passers-by, "You've never seen anything so beautiful in all your born days folks, Leonardo da Vinci's machine, only two dollars for as long as you like."

When the new year arrives, however, an immense weight is lifted off of my shoulders. The visitors to the camera dwindle to a mere handful each day. I tape the CLOSED sign up on the window whenever I feel like it, remove the journal from beneath my desk, and enter the camera chamber for hours at a time. All year long I keep these precious moments in the back of my mind, the light at the end of the tunnel. I experience a pure form of joy knowing that the rent is already paid, that the day belongs to me, not the tourists.

Last winter I began writing Vermeer. Though only in its early stages the research showed great promise, that Vermeer, like the Chinese and Leonardo, held a story from the pages of history, secrets which some library books alluded to, but that no one book fully explored. All summer long I anxiously awaited the first day alone in the chamber, the day to put into motion the fact-finding, the notes and discoveries I had compiled at the public library since last April. But this year the moment of fulfillment doesn't arrive. I sit inside the camera for two hours, as blank as the page in front of me. Every thought, every ounce of thought, sucked up by the woman from Florence. Her face floods over the camera screen, blocking out the ocean, a kind of eclipse which also seems to stop the flow of oxygen in the room. My movements appear trapped in slow-motion, and my arms feel as if they weigh several hundred pounds each as they rest on the railing that surrounds the camera screen, the screen that is now a black hole, a whirlpool, the beautiful face of a dead woman.

The felt tip pen point stands poised on the open page, bleeding ink in a circle. What can I write? Where is the first word? I feel it lurking somewhere, but all I see is the face. That face constricting everything inside of me.

So how do you do it? I mean, place a loved one out of emotion's reach, designate them a spot in your memory that won't hurt? A safe, secure place, where the past comforts you. With her I'd say the whole thing has to do with understanding the question, *why?* Why her, why decapitation, and most importantly, why the reccurring pattern? Why now after all this time? The police don't have a thing and could probably spend an eternity searching, because they're looking too small. The origin of this crime goes back way before any of them were born. You see, this is not the first decapitation in the history of the camera obscura. In fact, it is the third that I know of, to date. The third that I have thus far uncovered.

It sounds funny for me to say it, but when I studied and wrote about the other two decapitations I didn't bother linking them up into a grand crime theory. Many strange characters have used the camera throughout time, and I suppose I just read the word decapitation as a popular form of murder. I dismissed it as sheer coincidence. I mean one crime in China, centuries before the second similar crime in Italy, sure, both decapitations, and too, both involving inventors and innovators of the camera obscura. I guess it didn't strike me as that odd until the woman from Florence. But now, deep inside, I know that a dark force has reared its head. Coincidence no longer works as an explanation, though I want it to, believe me.

Half of me says to throw the whole thing out the window. What link? Pattern? After hundreds of years! You're insane, I tell myself. In hastier moments I even wish I'd never met the woman from Florence. I even wish I'd never poked my nose into all of those books. But is that rational? To stare this kind of evidence straight in the face and ignore it? Not that I'm sure I understand the evidence or what it adds up to. When I close my eyes and envision her beautiful face I know that I won't rest easy until I get to the bottom of this twisted business.

# THE STRANGE CASE OF DARIN

FOUR P.M., I lock up for the day. More clouds and fog on the screen. I can see out about twenty yards, just to the rocks that sit halfway between the camera and the cliffs. As the clouds pass overhead the light off the screen flickers in the room, like a television flashing in a dark living room. I pick up my pen.

As far as I know, the only other person who knew of the woman from Florence's obsession with the camera obscura is a young regular customer named Darin. Darin, a recent transplant from Southern California, who comes into the camera every evening for the sunset. He's a nice enough guy, an art student drawn to the strange beauty of the screen. Smart, yes, though he won't always look you directly in the eye. Physically speaking the boy is extremely skinny, and small, about five-nine, almost prepubescent looking, though he's twenty-two years old. He dyes his hair black, which looks highly unnatural, and very much like a kid who's searching for a strong statement about his own identity. I will entertain a conversation with him before and after he enters the camera. Occasionally he'll watch the ticket booth for me if I need to go to the bathroom. I can trust him with the money.

The reason I bring him up is that he did meet the woman from Florence. Well, *meet* might be the wrong word. He saw the woman in the camera chamber once when he had the day off from school. I'd be shocked if he mustered up the courage to actually speak to her. They were alone together in the chamber for a total of seven or eight minutes, before the woman left to go back to work. Shortly after that encounter he admitted harboring a schoolboy crush for her.

The events I speak of took place only weeks before the woman's death. I do not wish to imply that Darin might be considered a likely suspect in the case, and yet at the same time I want the inquiry to be thorough. My gut feeling is that he has nothing to do with the murder.

Other leads? Frankly, like the police, I don't have too many to go on, not if we're talking about apprehending a killer, cuffing and printing. Locking away behind bars. My investigation will follow a larger path. There is not one killer, there are conditions, reasons, and settings which are conducive to the crime. Yes, one man did commit this murder, and he's out there somewhere, at large. True, a killer must be caught, and the police will do their best, but what I will seek to uncover involves the root causes, the force behind a series of murders throughout time.

The woman from Florence's life was something of a mystery to me. There could have been dozens of lovers in her past, any one of whom dabbled in the world of the camera obscura, men who might be the killer. In the modern age the list of suspects might well extend to all photographers, all those obsessed with devices that evolved from the camera obscura, and considering the woman modeled most of her adult life for what must have been hundreds of artists and photographers, identifying the killer could be all but impossible.

# THE HIDDEN TREASURE ROOM

THE PATTERNS OF history are irrefutable, which is precisely what makes me nervous. History, without a doubt, remains one of my fondest pursuits, though I don't trust it for a moment, rather, I don't trust those who have written it. Certainly a distinction must be made between the actual events of history and the way certain historians might translate those events.

I will now recount the specific cases that involve decapitation, beginning with the Chinese. With my research on the Chinese inventors, conducted two years ago, located at the beginning of the journal in the third notebook. From there the inquiry travels chronologically, to Leonardo and finally Vermeer, whose story is still in progress, who himself might be involved in the case.

All of my research, my long hours of study, took place while sitting in a cubby-hole desk in the grand hall of the public library, an institution for which I have mixed feelings. If you realize that nine-tenths of what you'll read in that building is nothing but straight-out lies, then your time can be used wisely to extract small moments of truth which may prove valuable. But to go in *expecting* to encounter wisdom or the "whole story" translates into little more than an act of self-deception, an unsuspecting lamb to the slaughter. Still, in the library I read the following quote, which set everything into motion: "We owe our cameras of today to research conducted many centuries ago by two inventors in China, Mo Ti and Chuang Chou, men who laid the groundwork for the Europeans. Little is know of the two men apart from their eccentric scientific journal which dealt primarily with investigations into the behavior of light ..." This unassuming passage lit a spark in my mind. It was so simple, yet it alluded to so many possibilities. My hours at the library increased by leaps and bounds. Let us turn now to the product of my research.

The origins of the camera obscura, as I have said, begin in China, with the young philosopher/scientists, Mo Ti and Chuang Chou. The men were inseparable, best friends, colleagues, competitors. In fact they even looked like one another, so much so that people often got them confused. Both stood about five-eight, which was unusually tall for Chinese men at that time, with slightish builds, and, of course, black hair. Together they began experimenting with light rays and the bending of light rays when directed through fibers of silk. This eventually led to designs for a machine which they called The Hidden Treasure Room. Why *hidden treasure?* Probably because they thought their invention would make them rich.

The young men prided themselves on their spirit of adventure, as scientists are wont to do, and had become small legends in Guandong Province, known as ladies' men, because of their good looks and charm, as well as upstarts in the face of authority. Each held little reverence for their elders or peers, and while Confucian officials frowned upon this type of behavior, they turned a blind eye because the boys possessed such unique intelligence, the kind that might someday benefit the region economically. The truth is, when you've got a genius on your hands you give it some room to wander, let alone two geniuses. Don't the rules in life always apply differently to those in the know?

During the crucial moments of our story Chuang Chou played the part of the bad influence and Mo Ti that of the straight arrow. This contrast in styles gave their work together a depth impossible to attain from solitary research. It could have been the other way around, sure, but it wasn't. *Mo Ti* insisted on working late hours, while *Chuang Chou* preferred to leave the nights free for drinking. Both men, however, shared an arrogance, and a deep-rooted faith in each other and themselves, of the seamless path their lives seemed destined to follow. Work + Genius + Invention = Fame and Fortune. And for the most part nothing gave them reason to believe that the world wouldn't obey such a simple formula. The only problem, as they saw it, was how to get out of China, because China at that time was a sinking ship. Past the glory days of innovator, of untouched mystical paradise, the boys clearly saw the water level rising and began searching for life vests. "The corrupting Western influence staked its claim and China fell into the pool of isolationism," is one prominent historian's opinion. Mo Ti and Chuang Chou refused to swallow such a trend.

Close to the end of their work on the experiment Chuang Chou convinced his friend to take some time off for a vacation. The two ventured off on a long journey through the countryside, riding on a cart pulled by oxen, or perhaps floating by way of bamboo raft down the river, I can't find definitive evidence either way, but certainly it was one or the other. What did the landscape look like at this time? Pretty much the same as it does today: green grassy fields, mountains in the distance.

Dirty, hung over and hungry, the two young men eventually wound up in the village of Shenzhen on the South China Sea. They stumbled into a small cafe. Fishing nets covered the walls and a taxidermied giant marlin arched over the doorway to the kitchen. The two men chose a table near the front window, adjacent to a painting of a ship on the turbulent sea. An elderly woman walked out from the kitchen carrying a pad of paper and a piece of chalk. The men ordered mixed vegetables, noodles, two iced coffees and a bottle of triple-fermented rice wine, a specialty of the area, but the woman smelled alcohol heavy on their breaths. She lifted her nose in the air and motioned for them to leave. "I won't serve you, I'm afraid. You're already quite drunk. The first moment I turn my back you'll be gone without paying."

"We've got plenty money, lady, don't worry. You want us to pay in advance?" said Mo Ti.

"We're scientists, ma'am, from Guangzhou." Chuang Chou pulled out his travel papers and showed them to her with a mixture of boastfulness and authority.

The old woman apologized for her behavior, not that she could read the words on the document, but that they had a document at all struck her as very official. She rushed into the kitchen and returned with a bottle of the wine. "The food will be right out," she said, once again apologizing before returning to the kitchen.

"You know what I think?" asked Chuang Chou. "I think, to hell with Confucian approval. I think, no more worrying, no more waiting for orders. We can build the Hidden Treasure Room on our own. To hell with all of them. I didn't slave away on this project to get us some lousy plaque on the wall, or our picture in the Great Hall of Science. We could make some real money with this thing, we could travel."

"You don't think I know that already? Hey, if we could do it under the table, you think I wouldn't be the first one to say so? Because I would. Of course I would. But I really don't see much of a choice. Once we unveil it someone will for sure try and steal it right out from underneath us. We'd be sitting ducks. I'd rather have the security of the Emperor than let common criminals get their hands on it."

"We have to take it to the West. That's our only hope. There we can sell the ideas and become rich. Maybe we could interest the Italian. Can't you just see us relaxing in some plaza, drinking coffee, surrounded by Italian women?"

"I don't trust him," said Mo Ti, finishing off his wine.

"Why not?"

"Why should I? What reason is there to think he's any better than a thief himself? And there's something shifty about his eyes. Don't try and tell me you haven't noticed."

"Oh come on! What shifty? Look, he can get us out of the country, and pay us good money for our inventions. You've heard how rich the Italian churches are. I mean whole dungeons filled with nothing but gold doubloons and jewels. He's already spoken with me about traveling to Italy."

"Wait, wait, wait! What are you telling me? He told you what exactly?" demanded Mo Ti. "Why didn't you tell me what he told you?"

"Don't get defensive. He heard good things about the both of us, and mentioned a possible trip to meet the pope and the men of science in the Vatican."

"How could you not tell me something like that? I mean if I had someone tell me that we were going to meet the pope, don't you think I'd come running to tell you? Do you think I could even wait a second? Because the answer is no, I couldn't wait a second. So tell me, how could you not tell me?"

"I forgot until now," said Chuang Chou, looking down at his feet.

"You forgot!" Just then the door from the kitchen opened. Both men turned. Mo Ti put on his glasses, Chuang Chou knocked over his iced coffee but made no attempt to clean up the spill. There, in the doorway, stood a young woman dressed in a blue silk gown, carrying a large bowl of vegetables and rice. The old woman whispered instructions into the girl's ear that made her blush.

"Surely, this must be a dream," said Mo Ti. "Kick my shin, no, on second thought, don't kick it. If this is a dream I don't want it to end."

"I've never seen such a beautiful woman," answered Chuang Chou. "I know you've heard me say that before, but this time I really mean it."

The woman walked swiftly towards the table and set the bowl in between the two men. Both caught a whiff of her mysterious perfume. She smiled and sat down. The old woman brought a rag and cleaned up the coffee. Then she set two candles on the table, lit them and lowered the shades. "I'd like you to meet my daughter," she said.

# THE BEAUTY

HOW CAN I adequately describe the woman's beauty? Or, to put it into a philosophical light, can the beauty adequately be described with words? The beauty swells. The beauty radiates. It seems like it keeps growing with every passing moment. The longer that I don't see her actual face, the clearer and more defined it becomes, the more beautiful, like the crystallization of rock.

All the things I took for granted when she was alive, the line running from her cheek to her chin accented by the strong jaw bone, the playful curl in her hair. Little things, but the more I think of them not little at all. Details that now seem crucial, significant, without which you'd have no her. But if you're not looking, and I mean really looking, their utter uniqueness may not explain itself to you. I used to emphasize a *quality* which set her apart, but I couldn't really get more specific. Why? Perhaps I didn't know her well enough, or perhaps I wasn't looking in the right way. I remember one evening in particular, the second or third day after I had met her, when I stopped in at Pillar of Stone Bookstore, one of the few times I've ever been there, I should add, because of the feeling of the place. A corporate feeling, wall-to-wall carpet, office-like metal shelves. Anyway, I was killing time, browsing in the PHOTOGRAPHY/ARTS/CRAFTS section which I already have a problem with because the store alphabetizes books according to author, so that a book on Vermeer by Samuel Bronstein sits next to *How to Photograph Nude Women* by some guy named Brott, which in turn is next to a book on how to make elaborate paper airplanes by some totally irrelevant *B* author. But why I bring the whole thing up in the first place is that on the cover of *How to Photograph Nude Women* is a face which catches me completely off guard, a face which looks horrifyingly similar to that of the woman from Florence, and I know of course that she modeled for a living in the past. So I stare at the photo. All I can do is stare for maybe five minutes, perhaps even longer, and search for the quality that will tell me yes or no. But that quality never appears. So just to double check I scan the book from cover to cover, for a name, for model credits and the place where the book was made, which turns out to be Quebec. I know for a fact that the woman never lived or worked in Quebec, and I don't find an Italian name in the list of models, so I consider the case closed.

The point, however, is that if it were now, now that I can

identify her distinct features, now that I can name the quality with specifics, just one glance at the cover would tell me positively and definitely, *this is not the woman you're looking for.* It seems to me that what I've got is a double-edged sword, for my problems also start here. Today, everywhere I look I see the specifics, the quality: in the dense mist on the screen, or in the shadows etched into the cliffs in the late afternoon. But most of all I see her face when I close my eyes. Lines burnt into the insides of my lids, an eerie negative that I can't escape. Sleep doesn't come easily. Usually I resort to a few shots of whiskey, which almost always knock me straight out, but if it doesn't I'm in for a long night, a long, melancholy, drunken night.

## THE SEEDS OF BETRAYAL

CHUANG CHOU AND MO TI put off returning to Guangzhou for four more days, and ate every meal at the small cafe, talking to the young woman for hours at a time. Her old mother grew to like the two of them very much and went so far as to provide free meals on their last day in town. The two men simultaneously fell in love with the woman, and each knew that the other was equally in love with her. How could the other help but be equally in love? What was not to love? The doubt that remained was who the woman loved.

The woman spoke on her philosophy of time, on science, and on love while the two men remained silent, taking notes in their journals. They felt as if they were talking to someone from another country, or some different era, one more informed than their own. Someone whose insights on the world differed radically from anything they had heard before. She told them, for example, that she followed the doctrine of reincarnation, but added that time itself flowed both simultaneously and continuously, so that the past, present, and future really all took place at the same moment, only on different layers of reality. And this theory mixed with reincarnation led her to believe that she existed in numerous forms on many different planes of time and space, that reincarnation occurred all the time, so that one kept reappearing throughout history as a different person, or animal, or form of life. The two men didn't so much as squeak.

At the beach they took turns sketching her stunning profile. She posed on her back, arching her neck backward, accentuating her chin and razor-like jaw line. The two men scribbled, pretended to sketch, held out their thumbs in front of the paper for mock perspective, anything to keep the woman in such seductive positions.

Finally they told her about the Hidden Treasure Room, something they had vowed never to tell another soul until its completion. But hadn't the world utterly and completely transformed itself since they had met the woman? So much so that the old rules no longer applied? Their own vanity led them to believe that the only significant changes in their world would come about as a result of one of their inventions. Change was a consequence of invention. The woman, however, had existed long before she met the two of them. For years she had lived and breathed the thoughts that in a single night had completely changed the two scientists' understanding of the world. The young men found this a difficult concept to come to terms with. When they left the village they promised to return in two weeks' time.

On the journey home they talked about who loved the woman more, and why the other was not truly worthy of her love.

"I tell you what," said Mo Ti, "since you were so hot on the idea in the first place, why don't you go ahead and give it your best shot with the Italian. Convince him to take you to Rome. Make the deal with the Vatican and I'll stay behind so as not to get in the way. You know how bad I am when it comes to sorting out the details. You're the one with that kind of business know-how."

"No, no, no. I thought you said the Italian was a thief. Why the sudden change of heart?"

"I may not trust the Italian, but I do trust you."

"Well, I don't trust you!" said Chuang Chou. "Business know-how. I suppose you'd take a nice long vacation while I was away, right? Say down to the beach? A little town by the name of Shenzhen?"

"I don't know how to break this to you, but remember when you got up to go to the bathroom at lunch? Well, she told me quite confidentially that she didn't find you altogether attractive. Smart, yes, but physically she wasn't so inclined."

"You're a real dog, you know that? I'd sooner die a poor man than let you get a free shot at her."

"Come on, Chuang Chou! Listen to yourself. There's no

need to get nasty. I mean we both can't have her, it's got to be one or the other, and since you're the one with the Italian contact, it's only natural that you should go to Italy."

"I'm not going anywhere! Not until you and I return to Shenzhen and sort this whole mess out."

"Well, don't say I didn't try and tell you so."

"Tell what? Tell me what exactly, Mo Ti?"

"About how she thinks you're ugly."

"We'll just see about that, now won't we?"

# CODEX ATLANTICUS

HOW DO I come upon such an intimate knowledge of the young Chinese inventors? I read and I travel, in that order. First to China, many years ago. I spent months ahead of time researching Mo Ti and Chuang Chou so that when I actually got there I would have an idea as to what I might find. But all the reading and traveling in the world could not have brought me to the conclusions which I may now be arriving at. These hypotheses required writing.

They say that the best way to remember something is to write it down. Take the woman in Shenzhen, for example. I mean I've written down her theory on time and reincarnation a good four or five times, and I still don't quite have it. But every time I write it I feel that I'm that much closer to a full understanding. It brings up a philosophical paradox, one that I learned about from my father. Roughly it reads: if a person can always divide the distance between two points in half, then can they ever truly arrive at their destination? And of course the answer is no, and it seems to me that this theory applies to so many other things besides just distances, like history, for instance. In other words, a full, total understanding of the woman of Shenzhen's theories may not be possible, instead what counts is the feeling of having arrived. The feeling of understanding her role in the history of the world.

What I mean when I say writing is imagining. Not that the stories in the journal aren't true, because they are, but that when I write "Chuang Chou said, 'I've never seen such a beautiful woman'," he may not have said exactly that but only something to that effect. What's important is the feeling. Maybe I'll add a new word or two as my understanding of the story grows. But how many more words, how many new or different words will I need to add before the Chinese story feels done? Before I know for sure that the version is as close as I can come to the final evolution? At this point I'd say I'm almost there.

In any case, what's important, what's sure, is that none of this that I am telling you, the personal side, the dangerous side, ever made it to the pages of history. You only find that Mo Ti and Chuang Chou invented the machine, but never built one, or that Leonardo da Vinci cut open a human eye to build his own camera, and finally that Vermeer used the camera to trace his realist landscapes. But what you don't get, what has been covered up in a seemingly premeditated fashion, are all of the significant details that are relevant to the story of the murder. Take the library, for example. If I were to pick up a book on Mo Ti and Chuang Chou that dealt solely with their scientific developments (no dialogue included) without later researching the path their invention took after their deaths, then would I truly understand what they were alluding to, or what they were really all about? The luxury of the library is that it affords one the opportunity to follow up on ideas by cross-referencing, by tracing figures throughout history, so that at a certain point I can begin to understand Mo Ti and Chuang Chou conceptually, which becomes synonymous with or even better than the real thing.

Parts of the stories found their way onto the fifteen-minute audio cassette that accompanies the images on the camera screen. I recorded the tape early this year on my old reel-to-reel. It consists of music in the background and my voice in the foreground, explaining Chuang Chou's temper, Leonardo's genius, and Vermeer's dishonesty. Historical information, though I admit that since I recorded the tape my opinions on history have changed. I do plan to make an updated version soon, one which takes into account the recent developments and discoveries of the story. A tape which perfectly fuses the image and the facts.

The music deserves description, although I won't reveal my musical sources. It's strange, I feel protective of them, because of how fond I've grown of the way this particular music mixes with the images of the camera. I can't imagine hearing it in any other setting. It's as if the composers had the camera obscura in mind from the very start. "Suite for the Camera!" Long dark tones, ominous, sounds which make the sea feel like an enormous animal. Perhaps a cello, or a synthesizer programmed to sound like a cello. My favorite part is the windmills in the park. Crescendos in the music play with the speed of the turning blades, giving them a seemingly unstoppable momentum. I can watch the windmills all afternoon.

Before we return to China, let's talk more about the Italian woman. I never knew her name or her place of employment. I assume she had a job because she repeatedly told me she was on her lunch break when she visited the camera. There was an American boy in her life, that I'm sure of, because once I watched them kissing out on the cliffs, no mistaking her black and white checkered sweater and the shoulder length hair. The waves crashed below them, shooting up a dense mist all the way to the edge of the concrete path. I stopped the periscope from rotating and captured them in the center of the screen. They remained standing there, kissing, for only a short time, two or three minutes, before retreating down the path.

Watching them I became aware of a strange feeling growing inside of me, not jealousy or envy but rather a strong sense of disconnectedness from the events of the world around me. It seemed to me that the two of them stood on the other side of a vast ocean, that their lives had already been played out. That the drama originated from a script, and had been performed years ago. Standing there, I watched a video-taped copy, not the live events of less than a mile away. Like the disbelieving old woman that day in the camera, I couldn't make myself believe that for proof of what I was watching I only needed to leave the chamber and walk to the cliffs where, sure enough, I would find the young lovers. While lost in these thoughts a large wave broke against the cliffs and once more the spray lingered in the air, fogging the visibility on the screen. When the mist cleared the lovers were gone. I went back to the ticket booth and continued work on the story of Vermeer, but I will tell you about that later.

Three hours later she was dead, in the very same spot where she had kissed the man. I never saw him again. He could have been anybody. The cliffs are a good half mile from the camera, separated by a stretch of weather-worn terrain, so all I really saw was a figure, nondescript features, black hair, about her height. The fog was coming in and obstructed the view even further. For some reason I say American, call it a hunch, the contrast in their styles, their walks.

I've left something out, the head. The head to the body of the woman from Florence was never found.

# THROUGH THE PINHOLE

CHUANG CHOU MOANED all that week in his sleep, his dreams filled with the beautiful face of the woman in Shenzhen. He told Mo Ti it was serious, that this time it was somehow different, that he couldn't imagine how he could last another week without seeing her. Mo Ti thought quietly to himself, he paced back and forth and rubbed his chin. Finally he announced that he would not stand in the way of his friend's desire for the woman.

"You mean it?" asked Chuang Chou. "You'd really do such a thing for me?"

"Of course I mean it. I think she's more attracted to you anyway."

"No, you're just saying that to make me feel good. I mean last week,"

Mo Ti cut his friend off. "I know what I said. Chuang Chou, haven't you known me long enough to know when I'm pulling your leg?"

"Pulling my leg, of course! Well that's what I thought. I mean, of course, deep down it had to be that you were pulling the old leg, but you never can be too sure. So I ask you again, you were really pulling my leg?"

"It's the truth. Something tells me it never would have worked out between her and me. You give it your best shot, no hard feelings."

"I don't know what to say, you know I really just don't know what to say."

"Why don't you leave next week? I'll remain here so as not to get in the way," said Mo Ti.

"I don't deserve such a kind and understanding friend. Go home. Take the rest of the day off. No, take the whole week off. I'll finish up some loose ends and you can have the studio to yourself while I'm gone."

"Thank you. Perhaps I'll spend the time with my mother."

"Your mother? Your ailing elderly mother who loves you so dearly and who might not be around for so much longer considering her age? Mo Ti, who could ask for a more wonderful son, a more dedicated partner, a friend so virtuous?"

"Why thank you, Chuang Chou," said Mo Ti.

"No, my friend, thank you!" Chuang Chou threw his arms around his friend and embraced him.

Upon leaving the studio Mo Ti removed a letter from his breast pocket, the letter which the woman had handed him last week while Chuang Chou was in the bathroom. Written with a meticulous and delicate hand, it simply said, "Come back in one week, not two, alone." It took every bit of strength for Mo Ti to keep the note secret from his friend. He weighed his options. On the one hand, an unobstructed chance at the woman, but lying all the while to Chuang Chou. And on the other hand, guilt. Guilt Chuang Chou would no doubt subject his friend to if he told him the truth and showed him the letter. No, thought Mo Ti, I won't endure that kind of endless interrogation from my overzealous friend. Chuang Chou was the kind of person who thought that if he couldn't get what he wanted then nobody should. So Mo Ti chose the path of lies. Or, better put, that path presented itself as the one he should follow. Sometimes choice gets too much credit. More often than not the world presents itself in ways that make choice an irrelevant concept.

Meanwhile, Chuang Chou felt new life welling up inside of him. The vision in his mind's eye of the woman's body, of her skin unveiled before him for the first time, inspired him to work harder than ever on the Hidden Treasure Room. What part of her body would he touch first? Her hips? Or the shoulders? First, he would ask her to undress and sit down in a chair, so he could take a long look, so he could know for sure where to begin, the shoulders, or the hips, or the neck.

As he worked he heard the woman's voice, repeating the

theory that linked the past, present and future, and he wondered what sort of other incarnations his spirit inhabited or would inhabit in other times. And how did the Hidden Treasure Room fit into the puzzle? He imagined foreign lands, The Vatican, a trip on the high seas, a strong wind in his face as he stood on the bow of the ship looking through a field glass, searching for any sign of land. The woman wrapped her hands around his waist, and ran them up and down his chest.

For the next two days he locked himself inside of the studio. He reviewed his notes on the effects of light passing through fibers of silk, the way the light from outside redirectioned itself onto the white wall on the other side of the room, how the light formed the same murky patterns that he and Mo Ti had observed in the past. By what means could he change the focal point and bring the darkness into clarity? Suddenly he was struck with an idea: the field glass. He went to his bed and removed his linen blanket. With it he covered the window. Then he took a knife and cut a small hole in the fabric, so that light flooded into the dark room through the hole. Next, he picked a piece of paper up off of his desk and placed it directly on top of the hole. He brought the knife to the surface of the paper. His hand quivering in anticipation, the sharp tip pressed against the paper skin, all it took was a slight lean, an ounce of pressure, to make the small incision. He twisted the knife around and formed a neat circle of a hole, and when he turned around he let out a gasp of amazement. On the wall the once murky shadows now took on new definition. Distinctions between forms of light appeared, which shocked his senses beyond belief simply because he recognized the forms. He saw trees, and houses, and people, but the insane part of it, the maddening truth, was that they were all upside down. Chuang Chou ran outside, and then back inside to make sure that the images would not disappear. Elated, and mumbling to himself, he closed the door and headed in the direction of Mo Ti's mother's house. Could it be that he had seen into another layer of reality? One which the woman in Shenzhen had spoken of?

On his way he ran into the Italian. "I haven't the time to explain," said Chuang Chou. "Go directly to my studio. The door's unlocked. Wait there for Mo Ti and me. I've figured something out."

The Italian went promptly.

I'd like to add that this last segment of the story, the discovery of the first camera obscura, reads pretty much verbatim in two other books on the subject. One found in the public library and the other at Pillar of Stone Bookstore. The books themselves aren't important other than that they both corroborate the telling of this event. Not that they tell it particularly well or provide any real insight into the love triangle, which to my mind is a gross oversight. Furthermore, the books fail to research what became of the two scientists after the moment of their discovery.

# A TORCH IS PASSED

WHAT HAVE I learned so far from the story of Mo Ti and Chuang Chou? Many things. First of all, that the betrayal of a friend's trust is at the root of the problem, and at the heart of our story. Second, time, or better put, *timing,* is of the essence. And third, as I have said before, history is inescapable, better put, history becomes destiny, and vice-versa.

Did Mo Ti have any choice but to run to the woman in Shenzhen after listening to Chuang Chou go on and on about how he couldn't wait another minute? No, Mo Ti, who was also struck dumb with love, had to lie. Conversely, however, Mo Ti's actions really put Chuang Chou into his own kind of corner, they called his hand, as it were. I mean his best friend, lying to him in all of the worst ways, straight to his face. Maybe you don't agree. Keep in mind that these observations on the human psyche have less to do with psychology in the general sense than with the mental state of people involved with the world of the camera obscura.

Return with me now to China. Chuang Chou huffing and puffing. He ran through the front door of Mo Ti's mother's house bursting with the good news of his discovery. He called out, "Hello? Mo Ti?" No answer. "Where is everyone?" In Mo Ti's mother's bedroom he found a note next to her bed, on the night stand. The note read, *Mother, I've gone to Shenzhen for a couple of days. Whatever you do, don't let Chuang Chou know where I am. Tell him I've gone fishing with father. — Mo Ti.*

Chuang Chou's blood stirred and sped through his veins. His face grew flush, his posture stiffened. He strode into the living room, and from the family heirloom case he took out an ancient warrior's battle ax. He gripped the wooden handle and smiled because of how perfectly it fit into his hands. He sliced through the air with crisp, precise strokes. It was as though he had uncovered a secret reservoir of ability, and the realization made him all the more eager to confront his friend.

In part it was the blissful feeling that Chuang Chou found puzzling. Rage, he had believed, was an uncontrollable frenzy, not like this fluidity. From the moment he discovered that Mo Ti had lied to him, his body had seemed propelled by an unconscious force that gave his movements an eerie, smooth momentum.

Mo Ti and the young woman sat in a grassy field, underneath a cypress tree, eating oranges and sipping jasmine tea. The woman had laid her head in Mo Ti's lap and he gently rubbed her temples. Such a perfect moment, thought Mo Ti. Lost in romance, he didn't hear the quiet rustling of the grass behind him. The careful steps of Chuang Chou, as he made his way behind the tree. The deep breath Chuang Chou took as he positioned his hands on the ax handle. The two quick steps from the tree to Mo Ti's side. All so fast. The ax pulled back and already speeding downward. Bone breaking impact, a complete sever of the spinal chord. Mo Ti's head rolled down onto the young woman's chest, his face still smiling, still enjoying the day. She screamed, of course, then jumped up and tried unsuccessfully to climb up the tree, all the while screaming and crying.

Chuang Chou immediately surrendered the ax to Confucian officials and was imprisoned. As he was taken away, he pleaded for the woman to visit him in jail, but she vehemently refused, spat on the ground, and wished his death. Even so, Chuang Chou still could not help but feel absolutely in love with her.

You could say it was that final rejection that really crushed Chuang Chou's spirit. Wouldn't that type of rejection destroy a guy? Of course it would! Of course the look of disgust in the woman's eyes totally devastated Chuang Chou. Couldn't she see that he did what he did because he loved her? Or because of a force similar to love? Surely that was the only way Chuang Chou could describe the feelings inside himself. Something blind, a foreign presence deep down, and that presence, call it adrenaline, had emanated from the small moment of clarity he had witnessed in the Hidden Treasure Room. Somehow that vision gave Chuang Chou the strength to kill his friend, but how did it relate to his love for the woman? Why should the two acts, the loving of a beautiful woman and the killing of his best friend, be so intertwined with the vision in the world's first camera?

From his jail cell Chuang Chou informed the officials of his discoveries, which he now called The Locked Treasure Room, and insisted that they bring him his books. But by the time the authorities arrived at his studio the place had already been looted. Consequently, officials lost interest in the scientific knowledge of Chuang Chou. The great mind, the inventor of the camera obscura, hanged himself in prison the following week.

The Italian had wasted little time. Once he had arrived at the studio he shut the door behind him, locking himself in the darkness of the room. He turned and stood in awe of the images on the wall. After staring for a good five minutes he remembered his purpose and went to work. With great speed he tore down the blanket from the window and searched the studio for any notebooks or sketches. On the desk he found the large homemade book with the words *Hidden Treasure* on the cover. He crossed himself in the name of the Father and the Holy Ghost, and turned to the first page.

On a boat bound for Rome the Italian, the priest, held the books he had stolen from the studio close to his chest. A sense of great relief and well-being filled his mind, for he had succeeded in the mission on which he had been sent, to bring to the West some of the secret inventions of the East. His master would no doubt be pleased. The truth is that the young priest didn't know the first thing about spying or science or the Chinese. Simply put, he landed in the right place at the right time, so that on the boat ride home he allowed himself to believe all sorts of grand ideas. Surely, he thought, in the future the pages of history would hold stories of this trip, telling of the great young explorer who forever changed the world with his introduction of such an unusual new machine. For the rest of the journey he translated the book into Italian.

# CONCLAVE OBSCURUM

THE EVENTS IN China are pretty much wrapped up for now. Or are they? I will no doubt return to them after reviewing the cases in Rome and Delft. Perhaps another reading will turn up a new aspect of the story, a different angle, though frankly speaking, at this point Chuang Chou and Mo Ti feel pretty much nailed down. No one knows what became of the woman. Unlimited possibilities awaited her.

Today the sky is clear, and the view on the screen is magnificent, high visibility in all directions, a crisp horizon out to sea, excellent definition of the windmill blades. It was one month ago today that she was killed. The crowds that flocked to the cliffs those first days have gone now, the vultures.

Business has returned to the normal, winter pace, about twenty visitors per day. Most of them are tourists and have never heard of the camera obscura. French couples bumbling away about Leonardo as if he were from France. Really, the French try and claim him for themselves, the way they say his name as if he's an old family friend. Mention Leonardo to one of them and you've got yourself a sure ticket sale.

Let me tell you that while I do like Darin, the young art student, I feel I must divulge that the boy lacks any creative talent whatsoever. Not that I have told him or would ever tell him, knowing how sensitive he is when it comes to Art with a capital A. One afternoon he brought by some of his sketches. Naked women striking obscene poses, detailed drawings of rocks, and one of the camera obscura itself, done from down on the beach looking up. That last one, the one of the camera, almost made me angry at how out of whack the proportions were, the misjudging of every angle, the marred perspective and shading. I nodded as I shuffled through them, "Very interesting work," I said and handed them back to him.

In short, Darin sees himself as a genius, and is gravely mistaken about that. What he lacks is what every true artist requires, honest self-criticism. But Darin, poor boy, feeds his ego every step of the way. We're not all born to be Leonardos. He'll find this out on his own sooner or later.

To my knowledge he and the woman only actually met each other once, the incident I mentioned earlier, although he claims to have seen her at the camera "at least five or six times," which is absurd because every time she did visit I noted in detail the events of her stay. Therefore, Darin is only fooling himself with such absurd claims. You can see what I mean about feeding the ego.

I told Darin that I keep a detailed account of *every* day at the camera, not just the times when she visited, so as to avert his suspicion. Not that suspicion is even an issue, but an upstart know-it-all like him could take information of that sort, that I really only chronicled the days that she visited, and twist it all around into something that it isn't.

The police, he kept saying. You've got to give your journal entries on her to the police. It took a good long talking to before he was willing to drop the matter. It also took me showing him a phony entry to convince him that the journal contained nothing more than boring reflections on nature. Listen to this: *The fog sits out on the sea like a fortress made of cotton, the gulls seem afraid and hop from rock to rock spreading news of the coming gloom....* He even complimented me on some of the images, can you imagine? I glued the phony entry between the story of Chuang Chou and an exceptional piece in which I describe her shoulders and back. I left a book mark on the page so that when Darin came in to visit that day I could flip the journal open in a seemingly random manner. It worked like a charm. The rest of the journal deals solely with business trends, I told him. How many people and what kind, tourist, local, male or female. I'm no poet, I said, and pretended to be somewhat embarrassed at showing him the little bit I had.

To his credit, Darin really got me going on the idea of reviewing the journal for clues. Not that he knows about my investigation and that it might or might not involve him. No, what's best for Darin is to mind his own little business. If you really cared anything at all for her, like you said you did, I told him yesterday, you'll keep your nose out of the whole thing. The police are busy enough without some wide-eyed kid getting in their way. That really put him in his place.

Yesterday he actually had the nerve to tell me that he was in love with the woman. In love! He wouldn't know love from a slap on the wrist. What are you trying to tell me Darin, I said. I mean what could you possibly mean? Are you trying to say that it was love at first sight? Because we both know that you never saw this woman more than once, and for that matter you were in the darkness of the camera so you really didn't get a good look at her. Can you tell me what she was wearing? No, of course you can't. According to my entry, she set foot in the camera first, a good ten minutes before you did, and left, again, ten minutes before you. So let me tell you Darin, the green sweater and the long black skirt. And furthermore, knowing her, which I did a hell of a lot better than you I might add, she probably didn't even notice that you were standing there with that ridiculous look on your face which you no doubt had. Darin, I don't want you to take this the wrong way, but you're not exactly a prize for a woman of her caliber, you know what I mean? Why would she notice you? Why would any woman like that, from another country and all, give you the time of day? No, what I really think you're trying to tell me, Darin, is that you would have given your right arm for a date with her, not that you were "in love." Love requires some reciprocity, does it not, Darin? And with that, my final question for the day, Darin left in a huff.

Since the murder he's been wound up like a top. Usually I can count on his banality, his utter lack of emotional conviction. But since they found the body he's gotten all out of sorts and over-excited. Not that I buy it for even a second, that Darin actually feels any of the pain he portrays. Really it makes me a bit nauseated to watch him throw his tantrums, using her death to attract attention and sympathy for himself. That far away, on-the-verge-of-tears look that he gives. Really over the top, like an overacted scene from a soap opera. Has the man no sense of shame? We all feel grief, Darin, you don't have to wear it on your sleeve. It does make me wonder what he's up to.

One more thing about Darin, while I'm still on the subject. Because of his fascination with the camera obscura he asked all sorts of questions on the history of the machine, etc. Naturally I suggested the public library, but I specifically directed him to the books on astronomical uses of the camera, including the work of the "great" scientist Johann Kepler: star charts, celestial maps, etc. Books with which one might cure a bout of insomnia.

Darin first started coming to the camera before I had employed use of the soundtrack tape. By the time I made the tape I had grown to realize what an impressionable young soul he was and decided it was preferable for him to make a slower entry into the world of the camera. To this day Darin has never heard the tape. And though it's highly probable that he's gotten some bits of information in an art history class at school, to my knowledge he knows next to nothing about the true artistic legacy of the machine, at least he doesn't care to bring it up in conversation.

It's five-thirty now, so Darin shouldn't be here for another hour, which gives me enough time to start reviewing Italy and the strange case of Leonardo da Vinci. This story appears shortly after China, about one third of the way through the journal, notebook number five.

# CAMERA CLAUSURA

THE PLANS FOR the Hidden Treasure Room met with less of a splash than the Italian priest had hoped for. A month earlier, while the Italian was still daydreaming about his newly ordained status around Rome, British traders brought home the blueprints for a clock that they had obtained from another expedition into China. The Chinese, as well as inventing the camera obscura, had also discovered the world's first timekeeper, and these spies, the traders from Britain, flat out stole that idea and later claimed to have invented it all on their own. Such is the history of the world. Hence when the priest presented his great discovery for a room in which distinct shadows appeared in the dark, he received a chilly reception. In fact he was laughed at. Instead of being hailed as a miraculous invention which would forever change the lives of men, the plans collected mildew on a stone shelf in the Vatican dungeon.

Accounts of the story of the clock can be found in three separate library books: *The Timekeeper's Almanac, The Story of Time,* and *Affiliations.* Theft, plain and simple. When one historian says "bought" and another says "gift," you put the two words together and get "stolen."

The Chinese scientists' journal would have sat molding on that dungeon shelf until the end of time if it were not for one man, the man, Leonardo da Vinci. They don't come much more loaded than this one. And how could they? I mean he's in every direction you look. Say you're going to write a piece on medicine, he's there, or great inventors, again, he's there. Let alone art, I don't care, primitive, contemporary, modern, whatever. There's no ignoring the man. You can't not have an opinion on him, even if it's the wrong opinion, misinterpretation, or flat out ignorance. When you hear his name an idea flashes across your mind.

From my readings I've learned that Leonardo loved a good dungeon, and it was there, in Rome, in the Vatican, that for a short period of his life he was king of the best dungeon in all of Italy. A spiral stone staircase leading down to a magnificent if not ominous door. A door made of thick hard wood, reinforced with wrought iron trim, and in the center of the door, a large iron ring for those brave enough to disturb a genius at work. Inside, the room seemed to go on forever, partially due to the poor lighting, but also because the room was filled to the hilt with objects from other lands which blurred one's sense of perspective.

Given, as he was, free reign over the entire dungeon, it took Leonardo about a week to go through all of the junk the pope had lying around. Gifts from far flung destinations, occasionally a stuffed animal, or some art yet to be hung, not that there was a single spot left on the Vatican walls or ceilings to hang anything. By the end of his first week in residence he had removed only three items from the stockpile. A pair of gold spectacles, a three-cornered hat, and a book entitled *Hidden Treasure.* In this particular period of his life, Leonardo had secret pirate fantasies, not that you'd ever know it from his paintings of that time.

Leonardo worked on the edge, flip-flopping between two different kinds of activity. The first kind most of us are generally familiar with, the work done in his country studio, his painting, the Mona Lisa, the Last Supper, etc. Work with colors and light. But the other side was just as prolific, the world of the dungeon, the dark recess of a genius' mind, where no idea was suppressed, where experiments with the human body blossomed into a clandestine obsession. The truth? Leonardo lived a double life. Could you order a more perfect picture of a genius? Isn't that where the whole genius thing started in the first place? In fact every time you say genius, no matter who you're referring to, don't you also think about him? Even if it's only in a subconscious way? Like when I write about Chuang Chou and Mo Ti and I say "genius" to describe them, suddenly Leonardo's face comes to mind even though the Chinese came first. It seems to me that Leonardo invented the word.

At the time, no one had a clue that Leonardo did what he did down beneath the Vatican, nor would they have wanted to. Because after people have made up their minds about what someone is really like, say, "Leonardo is the greatest painter who ever lived," then they've made an investment, and will do just about anything to preserve the pure image of that person. I mean you could give facts, a signed confession from Leonardo saying, "I killed a woman," and still you'd have those who wouldn't believe it. They would claim coercion took place, perhaps someone drugged Leonardo, and so on. The point is, Leonardo used this kind of blind faith to his own advantage. And could you really blame him? No.

He played up on the whole brilliant thing. He'd tell his friend at the morgue, "Get me two arms and an ankle, and don't ask any questions. And another thing, I want the freshest bodies you've got. Nothing that has been sitting too long." So, sure, the friend gets the body parts, because maybe someday he'll get some recognition, after Leonardo finishes whatever masterpiece it may be that he needs the arms for. Perhaps Leonardo will dedicate the painting to him, or, better yet, name it after him, *Guiseppe of the Morgue,* forever carving his name into the concrete world of history.

Within a month he had turned the dungeon into a gruesome laboratory. He was not a tidy man. Body parts lay strewn on a wooden worktable, waiting in line to be opened up, examined, discovered. Hands, legs, elbows, all of them would eventually receive a chapter or two in his book on human anatomy.

Like most geniuses, Leonardo worked himself to the point of exhaustion almost every day. The routine went as follows: up by six, two cups of coffee with milk and sugar, then out to the country studio. The first model arrived at eight, his favorite model, who he would paint or draw until noon. Then a break for lunch, one hour, followed by miscellaneous projects until the next model arrived at three. Another session, which usually lasted until the sun went down.

When it was dark he returned to the Vatican, down the staircase to the dungeon, where he would work until well after midnight, drinking more coffee while dissecting chests or kneecaps, before collapsing with exhaustion. An inner alarm clock woke him every morning, always at the same time, and sent his daily routine into motion once more. As one might imagine, the routine began to take its toll on the man. Friends? Who had time for friends? Besides, what friend could keep up his end of the conversation? Whose two cents amounted to much compared with Leonardo's? No one's. Besides, the solitary life suited him just fine. What other kind of life can a genius have? What price genius?

# THE GREEN FLASH

WHAT WOULD I tell the police in the first place? Of course it was a man. Would a woman cut off another woman's head? And if I couldn't even tell you what the man looked like, because I can't, well, then what's the point of saying anything at all? Believe me, when I'm ready, when I've finished conducting my own investigation I'll reconsider going to them, but don't let yourself believe for a second that they'll understand a word of what I would tell them.

She was killed that day, the same day I saw her out on the cliffs with the man, the unidentified American man. Hence it is only logical to assume that the same man was the killer. Even if four hours had passed from the time I saw him to the coroner's estimated time of death, it would have to be said that whoever the man might be, he remains the top suspect.

It keeps coming back to me. When I watched them on the screen, that moment they turned and walked around the ridge, out of sight. He could have done it then. Hit her over the head with a rock, knocking her unconscious, then waited before cutting her head off. But waited where? Since the crime I've been to the cliffs twice, searched the grounds, and it's all pretty much out in the open. Someone would have spotted them for sure. The parking lot is too far away for him to have dragged her to a waiting vehicle. Perhaps they set up a second meeting, after dark. That's it, sure, when the tourists had all left. No one comes to the cliffs after dark, especially with the fog moving in. I left the camera at seven that night, late, because I found myself particularly engrossed in the journal. It was dark already, and so foggy that I couldn't see out beyond the water. For all I know he could have sawed off the head as I walked to my car. The idea makes me shudder.

It's now five-twenty, the sun rests on the horizon, but there's no sign of Darin. I must have really made him angry yesterday, because he doesn't miss this kind of sunset. When the sun is so clear that it almost seems to be searing the horizon with its heat.

Among other things, the camera captures an event seldom seen by the naked eye, the green flash. This phenomenon occurs at the very moment the last tip of the sun drops just beneath the horizon. Suddenly a brilliant green sparkle floods the sky for a mere second. The sky must be clear, like today, and even then one rarely witnesses this incredible sight. Together, Darin and I have seen the green flash a combined total of eighteen times. Of course, eighteen times means that I believe Darin on the occasions when he says he saw the flash when I was in the ticket booth or happened to blink at the wrong moment. Still, even without Darin, I have seen the flash a good twelve times.

The murder most definitely did not occur during a green flash. For the obvious reasons: one, entirely too much fog, and two, according to the coroner she died almost an hour and a half after sunset.

Darin, sensitive Darin. Remind me to take more care with what words and what tone of voice I use around you. Can you ever forgive me for the harsh way I spoke to you yesterday? Why must you blow everything out of proportion? Ah well, no green flash today, my friend.

## I SPY

FIVE-THIRTY, I close up the camera after sunset and head out to the library in the Valiant. I have decided to consult John Hammond's *A Chronicle of the Camera Obscura* for the street addresses of cameras located in Florence and in Southern California, where the woman lived briefly before heading North. I'm grasping at straws, searching for any possible clue at this point. Perhaps an owner of another camera might have some information.

When I arrive at the library the lot is full, so I'm forced to park on the street, three blocks away, right across from Pillar of Stone Bookstore. As I'm placing a coin in the meter, who should I notice walking into the bookstore but little Darin himself. So naturally I cross the street and enter the store, eager for a chance to see what the boy has been up to.

At first he's nowhere to be found. The bookshelves reach

from the floor to close to the ceiling, a good ten feet high, so that a clear view of the whole store is impossible. The shelves run in two columns down the length of the space, with subject indicators atop each one. The logical choice for Darin is PHOTOGRAPHY/ART/CRAFTS, located in the very last row at the back of the store, so I head for that sign, all the while getting angrier at the thought of it. I mean where do they get off? *Crafts!* The proprietor refuses to recognize distinctions between objects of beauty and those of ugliness, all the while claiming to do so in the name of some higher principle, call it egalitarianism, rather than for the base motivation so evident in every nook and cranny of the store, namely, sheer profit. Trash paperbacks or paper airplane books, each taking up space on a shelf which yearns for something better. But I digress from the story.

Before reaching the final shelf I stop at the SPORTS/HEALTH/FITNESS aisle. I hesitate, pick up a paperback and pretend to look for the index. Do I really want to see Darin right now? Now, on my way to the library? What if he insists on tagging along? What if he starts asking questions? "Why haven't you told me about this book before?" And suddenly I realize that Darin has never seen me outside of the camera, that he knows astonishingly little about my life when it comes right down to it. That he knows my address, but has never been over to my house, and that I go to the library often, but not the reason why I do. It strikes me that what we have is the perfect friendship, and do I really want to ruin this fragile balance right now, right here?

For the sake of sheer curiosity I peer carefully around the corner and immediately wish that I hadn't. The red binding on the spine of the book first tips me off, then the glossy pages, and finally an image of a naked woman. Darin stands with his back to me, flipping rapidly and then not so rapidly through the book, the book I recognize, the book titled *How to Photograph Nude Women.* Stunned, I retreat around the corner, sure that he hasn't noticed me, and turn and walk as fast as I can out the door. The coincidences most definitely do not rest easy with me, and now I can't deny the strange feeling that Darin is more deeply involved in the case than I had first suspected.

The results of my inquiry at the library that day provided precious little information. Florence no longer owns a functioning camera obscura. The last one, located on Palazzo di Inganno, shut its doors fifteen years ago due to construction of newer buildings that blocked the camera's view of the city. As for this neck of the woods, yes, another camera still operates down south in Malibu, located just across from the beach boardwalk pier. As odd as it sounds, the camera is inside a home for senior citizens. I have heard stories about this camera though I've never been there. Two things I'm not all that crazy about are Southern California and senior citizens' homes. Someone told me that to get inside the camera you need to ask for a key at the registration desk. That the place smells really bad, and that they're constantly misplacing the key. I understand that the view on their screen is nice enough, but nothing of the magnitude of my own camera. All of this data does not lead me to believe that the woman from Florence was a regular patron there. I can't square a picture in my head of that vibrant, youthful body standing in a stark, smoke-stained hallway waiting for a key, surrounded by so much decay. Frankly, this picture makes no sense. Darin grew up in Southern California, but where exactly? Malibu? Is it possible that he has been to this camera obscura guarded by the elderly?

## CUBICULUM TENEBRISCOSUM

TWO SHORT MONTHS of this routine brought Leonardo to a breaking point. The outward signs remained fairly well hidden from the world, but once inside the confines of the dungeon they abounded. First of all, upon entering the laboratory he took off his shirt and paced around the room half-naked for a minute or so. Then he put on the three-cornered hat and the golden spectacles and began reading *Hidden Treasure* out loud, to no one, while standing on a wooden stool. Where we enter the story he had already read through the book a good fifteen times.

He stopped dissecting bodies for a week in favor of reading aloud, until finally he came upon a revelation. That morning at five he left the Vatican, thinking about his favorite model, the one with the sparkling eyes. Book in hand, bare-chested, wearing the hat and spectacles, he headed for the country studio. When he reached the front door and saw his reflection in the glass panes, he confronted his own appearance for the first time in a long time. He stopped, and laughed out loud, a disturbed laugh, a laugh that might frighten you if you heard it. What was happening, he wondered, for he truly did not recognize the man in the glass, or, rather, how he had deteriorated to this peculiar state. Huge chunks of his memory hid themselves from him.

He retreated inside the studio, took a shirt from the clothes chest, and hid the hat and spectacles in the closet. "I am Leonardo," he said. "I am Leonardo."

But the book remained out on his work table, a thorn in his side, demanding attention. It wasn't that Leonardo didn't already know that rays of light through a pin hole could produce an inverted image on a focal point, because he did, he and others in Italy had experimented with the concept before. Rather, what increasingly fascinated him about the book were the drawings and illustrations by Mo Ti. Drawings of Chuang Chou holding up a scientific instrument, or long fibers of silk. Drawings of poor quality, and almost no aesthetic value, but Leonardo found something greater. One in particular, on page thirty-five, depicted Chuang Chou watching a beam of light hit a silk fiber and bend off in another direction. For Leonardo, the detail that disturbed him the most was the way in which Mo Ti represented Chuang Chou looking at the experiment. Dotted lines came out of his eyes and connected with similar lines that symbolized rays of light, which to Leonardo could mean only one thing, that the secret of the human eye lay within the camera obscura, and vice-versa. That morning he defined his goal: construction of a model of the human eye.

Leonardo jotted down everything he had felt and observed over the past few weeks in his own notebook. In fact, when he came to the observation on the human eye, he ripped out page thirty-five of *Hidden Treasure* and fastened it inside of his own journal. He finished writing at five minutes after eight, just as a knock came from the front door. The model! he thought. Oh, the model, my most favorite model in the whole world! The dependable girl whose face will someday come to represent the whole of fine art. The eyes that will humble all those who look into them. Thank goodness the model has arrived.

Leonardo got up and let the woman in, greeting her with the usual compliments. "You look so pretty today, don't you?"

"No," replied the woman. "Why must you say such things."

"Every day prettier than the last." The model began unbuttoning her dress, the red dress that Leonardo was so fond of, the way she always did in preparation for the day's work. "No, no, that won't be necessary. You can keep your clothes on. Today we'll be conducting a study of the head. In particular, your beautiful eyes."

"My eyes? You really think I have beautiful eyes?"

"Of course!" said Leonardo. "I mean, I know my eyes, and let me tell you that what you have here are a fine pair of eyes."

"But what is it about them that you like so much?"

"What is it?"

"Yes. Can you describe it?"

"With words you want me to tell you about them?"

"Well," said the girl. "Yes, with words."

Leonardo paused and took a deep breath. "How can I say it? Come here and open them wide so that I might get myself into a good position to tell you."

So the woman and Leonardo sit down close to one another and she looks directly into his eyes. Leonardo stares for a long, long time. At first the woman smiles and feels delighted to have such a soon-to-be-famous artist like Leonardo staring into her eyes. But then Leonardo's brow begins to wrinkle. Then definitely the brow furrows and hardens and the stare intensifies. Finally the stare turns mean.

"God, what's wrong?" screams the woman. But Leonardo doesn't answer and keeps right on staring her down. "Stop it!" shouts the woman, who can't seem to look away. Leonardo does not stop.

# TELL IT TO ME STRAIGHT

DARIN, I HAVE a hunch that something's not altogether right between us. And because I'm the kind of guy that I am, I'm prepared to make a concession if it will help alleviate our current impasse. If you say that you saw the woman more than just that one, singular time, then I suppose that under the circumstances I will believe you just this once. Say two times. Okay? Maybe once you saw her on the bus. Isn't that fair? You saw her twice, for the record. But if you're going to try and say more, perhaps five or six, or that you actually ever really talked to her, well then consider the deal off. The ball is in your court, Darin. This is what I will tell Darin if he ever shows his face in the camera obscura again.

The rest of my journal entry on Leonardo da Vinci reads quite predictably.

Leonardo stares into the woman's eyes for a good ten minutes, putting her into a trance state. At this point he can say things like, "Get up," and the woman stands. He retrieves the hat and spectacles from the closet and puts them on. Then, that night, under the cover of darkness, he leads her to his dungeon studio. Down the stairs, into the laboratory. "Lie down on the table," he says.

She drifts in a calm sleep-like haze because Leonardo told her that that's the way it feels when you're hypnotized. So she doesn't hear that he's at the weapons case, picking out which knife to use to cut off her head. Even if he can't explain it in words, Leonardo knows that there's something very unique about this woman's eyes. That if he's going to get anywhere with the *Hidden Treasure Room* he will require very special eyes, and freshness is a must. I mean take the Mona Lisa, in that one it's the mouth. You think he could have done that one with a regular mouth?

So he chooses a long, wide, Arabian blade, given to the pope by a traveling sheik. Leonardo fixes his spectacles and hat into place, sets both hands on the knife handle, grips, and raises it high above his head. All the woman hears is the sweet wisp of blade through air as the knife cuts down toward her throat. Such accuracy! Such artistry!

What Leonardo wants, of course, are the eyes, but in particular the left eye. Somehow it seems more suitable than the right. So he places the head in a wooden vice and starts in on dislodging the eye from its socket. He brings it over to his lab table, cupping it in his palm. Gently he sets it on the cutting board and holds it steady between his thumb and index finger. Next, he picks up the scalpel.

One singular incision is all it takes, straight through.

History lies unveiled. Leonardo looks at the inside of the eye and understands. He draws up the plans for construction of the machine that night, begins building it the following day.

The cold precision of the man gets to me sometimes. Not what he did, but how he did it. I mean the way life unfolded itself for him. He passed through with such ease, even on the verge of a nervous collapse. Was there ever any question of failure? No. A true legend, no other way to put it. Don't get me wrong. Yes, a murder was committed, and there's no excusing that fact. I suppose I try and look at it as a lawyer defending Leonardo might have. The "affected state of mind of the artist" argument. Inspiration is blind to a petty sense of morality. Have mercy on this soul! Try and see that what he did was for the greater good. Still, it doesn't help me like him, but I don't have to like him to appreciate his role in history. It does, however, diminish his irreproachable, almost saint-like status.

This is where the journal entry ends. The girl? Well, as I've said, he had a friend at the morgue. The girl vanishes, disappears from life without a trace. Who was she? Would it be callous to imply that her whole life represented nothing more than a waiting for that moment with Leonardo? If you ask me that's a compliment. And furthermore, that her life proceeded down the path that led to decapitation, that led to the secret of the camera, not to mention the secret of the eye itself, for a reason. That we might not have camera obscuras as we know them today if it was someone else, some other eyes. In fact, without her, whoever she really was, Leonardo might be remembered in an entirely different way. How many of us get to play such an important role in the history of the world?

Forget about any investigation linking Leonardo with the murder. This is one of the most respected men in Rome. When he tells the police, "She left the studio at twelve p.m. on Friday," they believe him. A guest of the pope no less. Accuse this man of lying, or murder, and you've made a serious offense to his high holiness. You might just as well call the pope a fool, or spit on his shoes. In any case, the pope would have had no choice but to absolve or pardon Leonardo as I have done. Only a few people in life can't be touched, da Vinci was one of them. How I wish the same were true of the woman from Florence.

Is she gone? Really gone forever? I'm afraid that the recounting of these stories has put me in a somber state of mind. The woman's face keeps coming back to me. Her curves, her radiance. A certain vigor exuded from her, one not contained by the physical border of a body. The air felt different when she was inside the camera. Just the sheer proximity of her made me more alive. Dead? Is she really dead? I believe it and then I refuse to. How could it be true? If I say it enough times, convince myself that she lives, it seems like I could really do it, really bring her back. Of course I know how crazy that sounds.

I realize now that I haven't given myself the proper time to grieve her death. How long is long enough? I must put down my pen for the day. I'll hang the CLOSED sign in the ticket booth and head home to relax and gather my thoughts. Reflection is a powerful thing.

# LOCUS SOLUS

WHEN I LOOK over what I wrote yesterday in my state of depression, it all seems very remote. Today I am seized with a sense of good feeling which bears no resemblance to the words of yesterday. Not that I have any right to feel good. Not that the investigation is turning up any great leads, or that the feud with Darin shows any signs of easing up. Perhaps it's just the fact the sun is out, and the coffee tastes just strong enough.

I can tell already that today will be the kind of day when I sit and stare out the window for hours on end. The kind of day when your mind takes a breather. Lots of doodles in my journal, no words, only shapes. Coffee, too, lots of coffee. By midafternoon I estimate five cups.

I turn around and look up at the Mona Lisa and realize that I'd almost forgotten she was there. Mona, always that quizzical look, the one which I have become so dependent on. Is it just you and me from now on? Fine by me, is what I say. Because Darin doesn't know a good thing when he's staring it in the face, and if he doesn't, well then maybe I don't want him hanging around anymore. But Mona, I'm afraid the girl might be a real stumbling block. Not that I mean that as an insult. Not that it wouldn't be just grand to spend the rest of time just you and me and the camera. Really, could a person wish for more than that? No. All I'm asking for is a bit of patience on your part, because, you see, if I don't get to the heart of this murder thing, if I turn my back on the whole issue, then I'm sorry to say that I might not be able to live with myself, let alone with you and the camera.

Patience, Mona, because there are signs of hope. With the rereading I have begun to add new portions to the story, not whole new chapters, nothing that you probably didn't know already, but bits and pieces. I promise to push myself so that by the time I get to Vermeer I'll be ready to finish the story and, in turn, solve the murder. Solve may be too strong of a word. At the very least I will put forward a theory as to the nature of the killings, which might be as close as we can get. Then we can put the whole matter behind us and get on with business as usual. Do we have a deal? I can tell by the glimmer in your eyes that we have a deal.

# THE MAGIC LANTERN

THE CASE OF the Dutch Masters revolves around the famous painter Vermeer, and takes place at a point in history when camera obscuras had been manufactured in small quantities. Astronomer Johann Kepler coined the term and laid claim to the machine as a "scientific device," though to me that misses the basic concept of the whole thing. In fact, that way of looking at it, that the camera merely captures nature, or reflects already existing beauty, couldn't be further from my own perspective. No, no, to my mind the camera *creates* whole new worlds. Vermeer shared my opinion, if I do say so.

A self-proclaimed magician named Cornelius Drebble, the man who discovered the submarine, owned his own portable camera obscura which he called "The Magic Lantern." Basically, it was a pinhole camera. He traveled the Dutch countryside, visiting small towns and rural areas where he charged a fee to gaze into his box of magical images. "Come forth and look into the past, the present, and the future. See the world of your dreams." Needless to say, he made a killing and became somewhat of a legend among the families of farmers. Couples offered him their beds for the night while they slept in the barn. Generally he received the treatment of a folk hero or wise man. Drebble needed that type of affection to counter his low self-esteem, the reasons for which I will discuss shortly.

After a typical two week road trip he would surface in a city to catch up on cultural events, and it was after a particularly long and lucrative journey that he arrived in the city of Delft. Without hesitation he headed straight for his favorite bar, which was always the first thing he did upon arrival in a big city, and ordered a bottle of wine. In Delft that bar was the Far East, so named because sailors frequented the place and donated foreign gifts after each voyage. Consequently the decor more suited an oriental museum than a drinking establishment.

So outstanding was Drebble's mood that he offered to buy the man next to him a bottle of wine. The man, who just so happened to be Vermeer, accepted. Together they drank a total of five bottles, and at dusk stumbled the streets of Delft singing songs about the sea, songs in which the sea doubled as a beautiful woman who confounded the most skilled of sailors.

They walked and walked all night until they crossed a

bridge over the Schie River (pronounced *she*), where they stopped to see the sun rising over the city. Vermeer lived in an apartment just a few yards ahead of them and was therefore accustomed to the view, still, he enjoyed showing it off to visitors as if it belonged to him. "Wait," he said. "Look at that. Have you ever seen anything more beautiful than that sight right there? Have you?"

"You think that's something? Well you just hold on to your hat." Drebble removed the bulky Magic Lantern from his duffel bag. "Here, hey, take a look at this."

"What is it? Are you a salesman?" said Vermeer, realizing that he had just spent the whole night with a practical stranger.

"Look at the sunrise through this. The Magic Lantern! You want to see beauty? Then look through here." Drebble held the cone-shaped tube up to Vermeer's face, pointing the wide end towards the city and the rising sun.

Vermeer remained silent for a very long time, and kept on gazing at the reflection of the city through the camera. "I usually charge people to do what you're doing." said Drebble.

Vermeer lowered the machine from his face. "Can you make me one of these?" he asked.

"Yes, I suppose."

"I mean bigger. A bigger one of these."

"Sure, other people have done it."

"Who?" asked Vermeer in an urgent tone.

"Astronomers mostly, rich people."

"Which rich people, and why?"

"Why? Novelty I suppose. You know you're awfully anxious about this," said Drebble. "Where do you want to build it?"

"Here, in my apartment." He pointed to the stone building behind them. "I have a view of the river."

"And why do you want to build one, if you don't mind my asking."

"Yes, in fact I do mind. Just tell me if it's possible."

"I suppose it could be done, that is if it's all right to tear the place up. There's a lot of construction involved."

"Of course. And I'll need a large screen, about three feet wide, and tall. Can you do it?"

"For the right price there are few things I can't do. May I inquire as to your line of work?"

"Don't worry about that. I have the means to pay you handsomely. When can we get started?"

"I'll need to sleep off this wine. How about tomorrow morning?"

"Fine." And with that the two men parted ways, agreeing to meet back at the house the following day.

What Vermeer saw when he looked into the Magic Lantern was a painting, but not just one painting. In every new direction he pointed the machine there appeared a new and more beautiful landscape. The way that the camera focused on objects at certain distances, but left others blurry, gave him an idea for a painting that had yet to be painted by anyone. He envisioned a new style, a new movement, one with which his name would be inextricably linked. So he strengthened his resolve. Could this be the break he had hoped for?

# CIRCLES OF CONFUSION

"ONE ASPECT OF Vermeer's work that has appeared to convince scholars that he did indeed use the camera obscura is his almost uncanny treatment of the play of light on textured surfaces. In the *View of Delft* and in the painting of the girl in a cone-shaped hat he has literally made light sparkle. And upon close examination the sparkling areas in each can be seen to consist of little dots of flattened paint called *pointilles,* which resemble nothing so much as the fuzzy overlapping sequins of light that appear in an out-of-focus photograph and are referred to as discs of confusion by photographers."

—*The World of Vermeer* by Hans Koningsberger

I use this passage merely to futher ground all of the statements I have made so far. Naturally, I found it in the public library, and public libraries across the country no doubt hold similar accounts, versions, and confessions of the story I am telling. Again, maybe not the exact story, the truth of the matter, but the clues, the basic framework. As I have said, search for the whole truth in the public library, and you'll be looking for an awful long time.

What can I decipher from this quote? Sure, there's the obvious, the "Vermeer must have used a camera obscura" part. But the words tell me this straight out, no inference has been made, I mean it really doesn't take a great intellect to read the quote and reach that conclusion. What interests me, however, is the line, "and in the painting of the girl in the cone-shaped hat," because honestly I hadn't thought about her again until now. The girl, the woman who lived with Vermeer in the apartment which overlooked the Schie river in Delft, his favorite model, his wife, she must have played a crucial symbolic role in the events which surrounded Cornelius Drebble's untimely death. I must take a moment to think about her role. Not that I don't already know what her involvement entailed. Frankly, she seemed somewhat peripheral when I first began the story, before I reviewed the Chuang Chou and Mo Ti. *Peripheral!* You can surely see how I overlooked the obvious. Embarrassing I dare say. I won't make the same mistake again, or at least one would hope not.

As for Vermeer, he painted nice landscapes, and women in hats, and fruit, but before the camera obscura there wasn't anything really going on in his works. Mediocre street-sold art.

"Very nice," was a compliment frequently used. Financially speaking he scraped by on a trust fund left by a great uncle, not the kind of existence you write home about. If it wasn't for the camera obscura the paintings probably wouldn't have gotten any better, and most certainly public libraries wouldn't shelve books entitled *The World of Vermeer,* rather *The Mediocrity of Vermeer,* or *More Boring Landscapes and Paintings of Fruit.*

## WHY OH WHY OH WHY?

FINALLY I GET fed up with the whole matter and I call him. He's not at home, so the answering machine goes off, or he is home and is screening the calls again. This is the message I leave for him.

*Seeing as you know how much I hate a liar, Darin, and seeing as how we have come to an impasse, either you are lying or I am, and I most certainly am not lying, Darin, well, then let me tell you that things have gone far enough. Not that I care one way or the other about this silly game you're playing, this silent treatment. What I'm saying, Darin, is that it's amnesty time. Time for you to 'fess up and tell the whole truth to everyone about you and the girl. That you never spoke to her, not that it really matters, but I think you'd feel a bit better about yourself, and you could put her whole murder in a bit of perspective, get it behind you as it were.*

At this point the tape beeps and the machine clicks off,

leaving me with a dial tone, so I call him back.

*Listen Darin, you can call me here at the camera, or come by for the sunset. It's been a few days since you've seen one. I tell you what, I won't charge you today. Let's bury the hatchet, what do you say? Look, if you really did talk to her, what did you say? Tell me that. Come down here today and tell me. Did you talk about me? It's embarrassing, isn't it, to keep up this charade. What's the point now? What's done is done. She's gone and there's nothing we can do about it. What do you want me to say? You want me to play along? Okay. So you talked to the girl. You did, you did, you did. Once, twice, however many times you say you did. In fact you met outside the camera. You went out for coffee and a movie. In the theater you felt a little nervous, let's say you both did, but slowly, mustering your courage, you slowly slid your hand down towards her bare knee. She was wearing that tight black skirt she sometimes wore.*

Click, and another dial tone. I furiously re-dial.

*What I'm saying Darin, is why don't you come down here yourself and tell me all about this supposed date? What is so difficult about coming the hell down here and letting me know what's going on in that little mind of yours? Why pretend that you knew her more than you did, which was not at all, and certainly not enough to kill her. You've been reduced to lies, threats and innuendos. Cut it with the police talk! If you care anything about our friendship, if you could call it that at this point, then you'll be here tonight. Good-bye, Darin.*

# SUBMARANICUS

POOR CORNELIUS DREBBLE. Yes, he was a wealthy man, still receiving royalty money for his invention of the submarine, and yes, the camera obscura gave him the opportunity to travel the country from end to end, but nonetheless he felt his life was incomplete. "For the love of a good woman," he would say. The sad fact of the matter was that he was extremely ugly. A large nose with wrinkles and creases and warts. Eyebrows thick and long which met in the center. An unruly case of acne which had stayed with him since childhood. The submarine came about as a way to hide himself from the world of women on land. In the depths of the ocean he could pose as a sea creature, a large rock crab or lobster. But that idea depressed him, because it was the final admission that life held nothing for him along the lines of beautiful women. No, he must trudge on and not give up hope.

Surely somewhere a woman waited for him, and this hope, this remote dream, became the sole tenet of his life's quest. So he sold the rights for the sub to the British, bought a camera obscura, and headed off into the country.

His fortune alone could have supplied him a mate, many were eager to get at his money no matter what the consequence. Cornelius Drebble knew that, but he was a man of principle, some would say faulty principles at that, in any case he refused any woman whom he perceived as chasing after his money. This resulted in years of celibacy and a weakening in moral resolve as the days went on. By the time he met Vermeer in Delft, he was just about at the end of his celibate rope.

The following day, Vermeer brought Cornelius Drebble upstairs to his apartment, which was plain enough by the standards of the time. A modest one bedroom on the second floor, with a living room in the front of the flat and a bedroom in the back, down a long hall, with the kitchen located in the middle, separating the two rooms. From his living room window the two men looked out at the sun rising over the city, just as they had done the day before. "Can we build one of your machines here, in this room?" asked Vermeer.

"No problem, I'm sure of it. You've got quite a nice apartment, the view really makes it," said Drebble, hiding his dislike for the paintings which littered the walls.

"Thank you," said Vermeer. "I live here with my wife."

"So you said last night."

"Did I? Funny, I don't remember."

"Sure, you went on and on about her beauty."

"Must have been the wine," said Vermeer.

"So where is she?" asked Drebble.

"In the bedroom, I suppose. Darling?" he called, then wandered down the hall. "There's someone I want you to meet."

Moving closer to the paintings Drebble noticed Vermeer's signature in the lower right hand corner of every single one. Cornelius Drebble let out a long disappointed sigh, for the mystery behind his new friend dispersed. He slapped his hand against his forehead. "An artist," he mumbled. From the earlier conversation with Vermeer he had filled his head full of strange and mystical thoughts. The man seemed so curious in the street and talked in such a secretive tone about the camera that Cornelius Drebble himself felt a part of some mysterious secret, a sensation he had not experienced since his work on the submarine some fifteen years ago. Perhaps, Cornelius had thought, Vermeer had an elaborate plot to conjure spirits, or spy on the neighbors. Perhaps Cornelius would not be able to keep such a tip-top secret to himself. Maybe danger, life-threatening danger, lay inside of his new friend. But the answer, as it had turned out, was no. Instead, Cornelius' mission was to build a camera obscura so that a second-rate artist could improve his paintings.

Vermeer returned with his wife, her hand on his arm for guidance, her eyes closed. She wore a long black skirt and a blue sweater. What went through Cornelius Drebble's mind at that moment is hard to say. Had he ever seen a woman of such refined beauty? No. No, he most certainly had not. Cornelius held out his hand, but the woman did not respond. Instead, Vermeer took his wife by the wrist and guided her hand into Drebble's. The two shook hands for what seemed like a long time, and Drebble realized then that the woman could not see.

"Blind," he thought. How many times had he envisioned such a situation? Meeting a beautiful, elegant, cultured woman, who happened to be blind. Blind to his ugliness. It was all he could do to maintain his composure in front of Vermeer.

"Cornelius has agreed to build a camera obscura for me here in our living room."

"What's a camera obscura? How big is it?" she asked.

"It's an invention which captures the beauty of the world inside of a darkened chamber," said Cornelius Drebble. "But no mere machine could ever contain a beauty like yours, madam."

"Oh my goodness! Thank you sir. Aren't you a suave one? What did you say your name was?"

"Cornelius Drebble, at your service,"

"All right already, that will be enough you two," said Vermeer. "Honey, you know we've got a lot of work to do, so, ah, if it's not too much to ask,"

"Okay, okay, you don't have to tell me to get out of the way. Very nice to meet you, Mr. Drebble. I'm sure I'll be talking to you again soon."

"Nothing would give me greater pleasure, my lady," said

Drebble as he bent to kiss her hand.

"Such a charmer!" said the woman, who smiled and walked down the hall.

After the woman left the room Vermeer took a serious tone. "Listen Drebble, I know how men are, I'm one of them myself, and I expect that kind of behavior from them, but a word to the wise. Keep your mind on your business and off of my wife."

"Sir, may I remind you that I don't need this kind of lowly employment for my well-being. In fact I do it only as a favor to you, a struggling artist, so that you might paint your landscapes, your fruit bowls, with a bit more clarity. Yes, your wife is beautiful, a person would have to be blind himself not to notice, but in no way am I in the least bit interested in her."

"Glad to hear you say it."

"Now, before we begin, I'd like a down payment as a show of good faith, and an apology for the implication you made just now concerning your wife."

"I'm sorry, really, I don't know what came over me. You see she's just such a sucker when it comes to that chivalry crap and you were laying it on pretty thick. Look, I get kind of protective with her, forgive me." Vermeer excused himself, went to the bathroom, and shortly returned with a palm full of folded bills.

"Forgiven," said Drebble.

# ONCE IN EUROPE

THE FOG HAS saved Darin tonight. I can't logically blame him for not showing. The screen is impacted with gray shadows. Not that the sight isn't a beautiful one, really I almost prefer it that way. The slowly shifting marbleized patterns of fog on the dark screen give one the sensation of peering into a never-ending void. But Darin only acknowledges the value of clear days, which only goes to show how shallow the boy really is.

I don't know what happens to me when the fog first hits, that is to say what used to happen and what I hope will start happening again. My mind draws a blank, I sputter to a halt. I'll have been concentrating on the story, writing intently, while the sun shines over the cliffs, and the next thing I know there's a stiffness in my arm and I can't think of the next word. Then I notice that the fog has encroached on the shore and it all makes sense. I give myself a good half an hour to rest and readjust to the new climate prior to returning to the page. But here's the thing, the writing changes. Before the fog, the story will more often than not read happily, a love story, a success story, but after I return from my break, events turn decidedly sour.

This circumstance can manifest itself in subtle ways, say the lively character grows ominously silent, or a cat gets run over by a car. But more often than not it comes out in dramatic fashion, murder, etc. My mind chooses to concentrate on the darker side of history, and even if I wanted to, I couldn't focus on the happier times, the good.

On the night the woman from Florence was killed the fog came in like a brick wall. I was working on the Vermeer piece. I can't help but remember feeling particularly disturbed after I had laid my pen down. For the first time I felt as if what I was writing had grown somehow out of my control. I looked down at the ink on the page, the words, and felt totally detached, even surprised at what the words said. Was Vermeer acting how Vermeer really would have, or did in fact act? And if so, then what was I to decipher from his insanity? But now I'm jumping ahead. I mean I don't want you to think that any of Vermeer's actions up to this point could be termed insane. The insanity I refer to follows shortly.

That night I left the journal underneath my desk in the camera, deciding it might calm me down to have a night away from it. I walked to the car, which was out in the lot beyond the cliffs. As I have said before, it must have been at that precise time that the murder took place. The writing had affected me so much that I don't remember thinking or hearing anything on that walk. My mind lingered on Vermeer's wife and the plight of the blind.

I decided to give the library a miss, seeing as it was already very late, and drove straight to my apartment. When I arrived home I went into the living room and took out my old photo album from the bookcase. The trips to China, Rome, and Amsterdam. How many times had I looked at those same pictures with more or less the same feeling? The sentimental yearning for times long past, the flash-backs. But now, I know it sounds crazy, it was as if I had never been to those places. Pictures of me shaking hands with Italians at the Vatican gates, men I couldn't remember. One of a man hugging me like I was his most trusted friend, and there I stood hugging him back! Again, my mind drew a blank. Then I came to a photo taken in Delft, of Vermeer's old apartment. My hands began sweating, and I couldn't hold the picture still. There, in the right hand corner, walking down the sidewalk along the Schie River, was a woman carrying a long red and white blind-man's cane. Her straight black hair obstructed a clear view of her face, but she wore a long black dress, similar to one that I had seen the woman from Florence wear. Was I losing my mind? I swear to you, God as my witness, that she wasn't there before, or I didn't notice her. But I still maintain that I didn't notice her because she simply wasn't in the photo. So what I do next comes in a fit of confusion and paranoia, because there's no logical way I can explain what I have seen though I try and try. I picked up my cigarette lighter and burned the photo. And the second after the last bit of picture shriveled in flame, I wished I hadn't done it. Deliberately destroying my links to the past, what a stupid, stupid thing to do!

Sleep, I tell myself, but all that night I lay awake thinking about Vermeer, the woman from Florence, and the photograph. It's not me, it's the camera. Look at its history! After I reconciled myself to this fact I fell into a deep sleep.

When I arrived at the camera the next day, police had taken over the parking lot and taped off the entrance to the concrete path. I parked the car down at the beach and ran up the hill to the camera. Once inside I focused the periscope on the forensic team at Lookout Point. With a sense of horror I watched them load a body bag onto a stretcher. A large dark spot soiled the concrete, blood no doubt. A knock came from the door, and I answered to find Darin standing motionless, as white as a sheet.

He began babbling about the murder. Just yesterday, he said, I was out on the cliffs, right there, at Lookout Point, can you figure? They say the head is missing. How could something so horrible happen, just last night, when only yesterday I was standing right there, right there I tell you!

Get a hold of yourself, I said. What were you doing out on the cliffs anyway, Darin? I said.

And here is what Darin tells me. Darin says that he was out

there at Lookout Point with the woman from Florence. That he just happened to be on his way to the camera obscura when he saw the woman standing alone on the cliffs, so naturally he decided to stop and chat.

Okay, Darin, calm down. Calm down, little flower. Yes, it certainly is most horrible that a murder took place in our neck of the woods, but that doesn't mean we have to loose our grip on real events. You want me to believe that the man I saw her with yesterday, because I did see her on the cliffs in the late afternoon, wasn't really an American boyfriend, but was in fact you? Not that I could for sure see that the man on the cliffs wasn't anyone specific, that physically speaking, perhaps as far as body types go, you might or might not fit the description. Because to tell you the truth, Darin, I didn't get a clear enough look. But for reasons of pure logic I'd have to count you out of the running. First of all, Darin, why were you en route to the camera when you could see with your own two eyes that the fog covered the horizon out to sea, hence eliminating the sunset? And second, why wouldn't you have come in and said hello if you were in the neighborhood? And third and most importantly, Darin, the man I saw yesterday kissed the woman from Florence square on the mouth. So I put it to you, Darin, why no mention of a kiss? No, no, too many unanswered questions spoil what might otherwise have been a nice little fantasy.

Go along to school my boy, and stop all of this silly talk. I know it's not every day that there's a murder and I know you want to be involved and everything, but you've got too many holes in your story.

Pesky Darin, all the while arguing, spitting back his story as if it were the truth. Don't listen to me then, Darin. You believe what you want to. If you say that the earth is flat, well then I suppose the rest of us have no choice but to believe you. Enough for today, Darin. Go on off to school, I said. So Darin left, still claiming to have been with the woman.

Within an hour most of the police were gone, but reporters and tourists still lingered at the scene. The woman from Florence should be arriving at any time now, or so I thought. Then it hit me, an overwhelming wave of nervousness. The head, you idiot! How could I have be so oblivious to the events around me, another decapitation! Just the day before hadn't I been hypothesizing on the death of Cornelius Drebble? His untimely murder? Of course I had. And wasn't it in the back of my mind that Vermeer would have no choice but to chop Drebble's head off for a reason that hadn't yet presented itself? It was, it was. Suddenly the words in the journal had turned on me. Before, I always found solace and distance from the people and events involved in the stories. But now, with the photo in Delft, and the beheading on the cliffs, that world of the past stalked and invaded my present-day existence. History itself had come to the present to confront me. Surely it made me write these stories, it must have. How else can I begin to explain such events? It led me here, whispered its secret into my ear, and now waited for my reaction.

I am not a spiritual man, but I turned to the Mona Lisa and prayed. Woman from Florence, I pleaded, deliver yourself promptly to the camera. Please show me that your beautiful head still rests safely upon your shoulders. A fruitless prayer. Two hours later the afternoon newspaper confirmed the identity of a young Italian woman from her fingerprints, though no name was released at that time.

I found the story on page three, and it wasn't until the fourth or fifth reading that I reacted to it in any emotional way. At first the words only provided a surface meaning. I read them as a string of symbols, distant and devoid of life. Yes, a murder had taken place the night before. That what we were dealing with was an unusual homicide, a decapitation, and furthermore, that the head had not yet been recovered. Police investigators had not put forth any theories as to the possible motive.

The article took up only two small columns, each three paragraphs long. The style read fluidly and conveyed the information with little appreciation for detail other than the word unusual.

But the more I read it, even the simplest and most nondescript of words began to take on inflated qualities, and the murder itself, what it must have been like to watch, appeared in my mind's eye. The grisly words that the reporter purposefully suppressed now came from the page in startling clarity. I read it over and over, first to myself and then out loud. Finally I took the paper with me into the camera chamber and read by the light of the image on the screen.

What started out as a series of isolated still pictures in my mind became, with each new reading, a blow-by-blow account of a blade cutting through her neck, a live, animated view. The rotating image of the camera screen seemed to speed up the frantic pace of my imagination. I grew dizzy, and grasped the hand rail of the screen as a wave of nausea rose from my stomach. The cold stainless steel blade falling out of the sky towards the pulsating jugular taut with blood, a neck, arched back and innocent. The gash bursts through the skin unleashing a geyser of blood and human fluid shooting all over the pavement. A loud snap from the vertebrae.

Abruptly, a stray tourist pushed his way through the customer door, filling the chamber with light, exploding my horrific vision. "Are you okay?" he asked.

Since those first, and most confusing hours, my mind has had a chance to calm down. There's no blood on my hands. First and foremost I am innocent, and the knowledge of this has given me the distance I need to do the work which needs to be done.

What got me started on re-telling the events of those horrible days? Ah yes, the fog, and the same kind of fog has rolled in tonight. Darin is still nowhere to be found. I imagine he's fixing all of the ludicrous details of his story. Persisting with his warped version of events. I'd like to see him here now, spouting off his fiction, if only for the sake of marveling at how a man can live in such a deluded sense of reality.

# THE RIVER SCHIE

EVERY NIGHT BEFORE bed Vermeer told his wife how truly ugly, ugly, ugly Cornelius Drebble was to those who could see him. How it pained him to have to work a good portion of the day with a man so ghastly ugly. And every time he would go into such a tirade his wife would reply, "He seems like such a nice man," and "How can you judge him on his physical appearance alone? Aren't you ashamed of yourself?" These responses only prompted Vermeer to lash out more vigorously than the time before.

"Perhaps he's the ugliest man alive!"

"I don't believe you," she protested.

"Why would I lie to you my darling? It's the plain and simple truth. I assure you, if the man was bestowed with good looks

I'd be the first one to tell you so. But the facts speak quite to the contrary."

"I'm tired of this conversation. Let's go to sleep," she said and rolled over. Every night the same routine, for over three weeks.

Construction of the camera took just one month. On the back wall of the room a square screen made of canvas hung from the ceiling. Walls were built over the windows to keep light out of the room. A small hole in the center of the wall let light pass through one of two special lenses, which Drebble had ordered from Amsterdam.

Vermeer began tracing the painting *View of Delft* immediately. With a pencil he followed the lines of the river, the city gates, the sky. So easy, he thought. The rest was paint by numbers. He spent hours in the darkened room every day, more than he had ever spent painting in the past, producing far more work than he ever thought possible. Before the camera obscura, it took him weeks to complete a single landscape. Now he could make four or five in the same amount of time. And the paintings themselves! The paintings bore a realism, a style so much more vivid than the old ones. Perspective unfolded in a whole new way. Certain areas of the canvas seemed to glow with light, while others he purposefully left blurry, portions in the foreground, and wasn't it only logical? Wasn't that how the eye saw the world, both in and out of focus simultaneously? So why did he feel that he was committing a kind of crime against the truth when he painted blurry sections of the canvas?

Only one problem with the whole scenario, thought Vermeer. What if the world found out that he used the camera for his paintings? Would they value them as highly? Of course not. And wouldn't every artist in town go and build their own cameras? Yes, yes they would. So maybe that unique quality could be passed off as a technique instead of the work of a bona fide genius. Very troubling indeed.

Immersed in his new work, and convinced that he would soon be famous, assuming he could solve that one little problem, Vermeer missed all of the little signs that his wife had slept with Cornelius Drebble. A secret lunch here, a rendezvous for coffee, love poems recited in the countryside, all of these events snowballing into a torrid afternoon of sex in Cornelius Drebble's hotel room.

Cornelius had not had sex very often, twice in fact, but this did not mean he was not knowledgeable on the subject. Throughout his life he had read the erotic journals of the most admired sexual personalities history had to offer, so that when the time came, and it most certainly had come, he would not fail to please his lover.

Poor Vermeer! Deceived so. At night he apologized to his wife for working so much, but said that soon they'd have all the money they could count, and could spend every second of the day together. "This time I mean it," he said. "But what did you do today, my darling? Tell me what you've been up to."

His wife's response began to frighten him. "Nothing," she said rolling over to sleep.

No matter, he thought. I know it must be hard on her, but if I devote myself to my work now it will surely pay off for the both of us later.

# LOOK AT IT THIS WAY

THE WOMAN FROM Florence could see. She wasn't blind. Plain and simple. Let me say that I couldn't leave something like that out even if I wanted to. She came to the camera without using a blind-man's cane, and stared at the screen with two perfectly functioning eyes. If any doubt as to the issue has surfaced, please, put it to rest.

Look, I'm not saying I've got a neat little explanation for the photograph, and doesn't it tell you something about the kind of man I am that I can come out and admit it? But if you have to have an explanation, if you can't sleep not knowing *Why a blind-man's cane? Why that black dress?* I suppose I can supply you with some possible answers.

Most obviously, the dress. Women all over the world wore versions of the dress. The dress appeared in fashion magazines in most European countries, so why not the dress? You really can't get too far with something like clothing.

The blind-man's cane certainly presents the greater problem, because I do consider myself a person with an eye for detail, and in no way, shape, or form do I recall the cane in the photo before that night. What I'm going to enter into the record at this time could be called food for thought. Not that I'm asserting this as the way it actually happened, rather as an example of how these days almost anything is possible.

Just yesterday by pure chance I passed by Pillar of Stone Bookstore and happened to glance in the window at the rack of magazines. And there in the front row, on the cover of *World Photographer* I read the headline, "Re-inventing the Photograph: Computers Construct New Reality." So, of course, I stop, go inside and read the article, because at this point I'll take anything I can lay my hands on.

The article tells me that a person like you or me now has the ability to alter history. It states that I could bring down my old family photo album to a man with a very sophisticated computer, give him the photos, and say something like, "Erase Uncle Gerry from all of these pictures." Or, if I'm really feeling adventurous,"Why don't you do a photo with me and that famous perfume model, make it so that we're holding hands underneath the Eiffel Tower." I'm not exaggerating. They can actually draw objects or people into your old photos, and then shoot out new negatives so real, so convincing, that there's no way to know the truth.

The point isn't that someone broke into my house, got a hold of my photos and rearranged them with some computer, though I admit it's a possibility, a remote possibility. The point, with all of its terrifying implications, is that photos don't prove anything one way or the other. I bought a copy of the magazine, clipped out the article and glued it into my journal to make that very point.

# WILL THE REAL DARIN PLEASE STAND UP?

VERMEER, THAT RAT, that snake in the grass. The money he gave Cornelius Drebble for the down payment was not his to give. He stole it from his wife's inheritance money, hidden underneath a loose floorboard in the bathroom. Truth be told, Vermeer had been paying the bills with the money for months, and lying to his wife about paintings he had never really sold. You could say, as it has been said, that the camera obscura merely represented a get-rich scheme for a man whose ship was about to sink.

I go back and forth. Sometimes I see him as victim, and other times I say to myself, live by the sword, die by the sword. Vermeer lived in a deluded reality, envisioning riches and fame while stealing from his wife. He promised to pay Cornelius Drebble with money he never had but would possibly acquire with the sale of his new masterpieces. Fortunately for Vermeer luck handed him the camera obscura, which probably was his only real hope.

When he sold his first camera-aided painting for the equivalent of one hundred dollars, only five dollars remained hidden underneath the bathroom floorboards. Most certainly Vermeer narrowly avoided disaster with his wife, or should I say *postponed?*

In some ways Darin reminds me of Vermeer, or vice-versa, and in some ways I see him more as a Cornelius Drebble. Luck, yes, struggling artist, yes, but Darin won't ever achieve fame, that's for sure. And as for Cornelius Drebble, Darin lies when he shouldn't. Ugly, that too, and he probably hasn't had sex more than once or twice, but somehow I just don't see him getting to sleep with the blind woman, or the equivalent of the blind woman. It seems that Darin has inherited all of the negative characteristics without the rewards of fame or wealth or sexual fulfillment. In my mind that makes for one frustrated Darin.

Three days gone by, three evenings with clear skies, three nights since I left the message on Darin's machine, and still no show. What's going through his mind? What could possibly be going through that little peanut of a brain? Does he think I don't know what he's up to? I know a game when I see one, Darin, when I'm smack dab in the middle of one. Suspiciously silent so as to make me think he really did meet the woman that day and at the very spot where she was murdered. That somehow he can't bear to go outside, or call anyone, because the pain, the grief, overwhelms him so. Isn't that it? What else could it possibly be? The other scenarios are so far-fetched I don't think they deserve consideration. That maybe Darin thinks I know something, or that I'm somehow involved. Absurd, I'm sorry I brought it up. How about this one? Darin wants me to think that he himself had a role in the murder. Ha! That his involvement with the woman had gotten out of hand. Not that she cared for him, because, well, for obvious reasons this just isn't in the realm of possibilities, but that he had gotten so out of whack that he did something. He watched her get killed, or he paid someone to kill her, or I don't know what, because he loved her more than anything in the whole world, but she absolutely and categorically wouldn't give him the time of day. Possessed by love, he had a hand in the murder. Is that what you really want me to think? Not that I'm dumb enough to actually go for such a story in the first place, but is that what you actually want me to think? You know you're doing a pretty good job making yourself look like the killer. Boy moves from Southern California to attend art school coincidentally at the same time the woman from Florence also arrives. Boy obsessed with the camera obscura. Boy admits to being "in love" with said woman. Boy's behavior changes erratically after the woman's murder. Not a bad case you've constructed around yourself, but let me lay it out on the table for you, Darin, you don't have what it takes to commit a crime of this magnitude. The intelligence, the wit, the creativity, you name it! The one thing that gets me though is why you'd want me to believe you killed her in the first place. Do you think I'll respect you more? Well you're wrong. I don't respect Leonardo more, or Chuang Chou, so why would I respect a talentless adolescent like yourself? Enough with the games is what I say, enough already!

# FAME, FORTUNE

VERMEER SOLD FIVE of the camera obscura-aided paintings almost immediately, all of them landscapes of Delft and the surrounding countryside. Half of the money he gave to Cornelius Drebble, who had literally forgotten about the debt because of his love for Vermeer's wife. Vermeer made sure that Drebble gave him a handwritten receipt so that there would be no question as to the resolution of the payment. But what did money matter to Drebble? Hadn't working on the camera obscura enabled him to sleep with the woman of his dreams? It had, it had. And wasn't that payment enough, even if Vermeer might not want to hear it put in those terms?

Lovesick Cornelius Drebble convinced himself that he had found true love and everlasting happiness. Poor lovesick Cornelius Drebble! Vermeer's wife did enjoy his company, true enough, but really, after that one, singular time, that moment of passion, her desires had greatly subsided. The woman, for as long as she could remember, had dreamt of such an encounter, but in her dreams were expressly written the provisions of a *brief* and *secret* affair. Hence, once the deed had been done, the act, she felt content to return to the bond of wedlock. Remorse? No. A bit uncomfortable in bed that first night, but really the woman felt refreshed, if anything.

So Cornelius Drebble kept on with his own assumptions of true love, and Vermeer's wife kept on with hers.

The night after Vermeer paid Drebble the rest of the money he owed, he lay down in bed a new man, a man on top of the world. "Well, happily, my darling, I can report to you today that progress abounds. With the sale of my recent works I managed to pay our ugly friend the last of the money."

"I suppose that means he'll be on his way then," she said.

"I would think so. Off into the forest to perform his magic tricks for the farmers, or whatever it is that he does."

"He is a very strange man," she said. "Though I did grow to like him, the little that I talked to him, that is."

"Strange and ugly, my darling. Really you must thank your lucky stars that you never did lay eyes on him," said Vermeer. "Darling, tell me that you love me. I haven't heard you say it in such a very long time."

"Yes, of course I love you. How could I possibly not

love you?" she replied.

"I just needed to hear you say it. Now, darling of mine, I need to ask you a favor. A very important favor concerning the camera obscura."

"What is it then?"

"I'd like that to be our little secret. What I mean is, please, darling, don't tell anyone about it, okay? Do you think that would be all right, my sweet?"

"Well, whatever for?"

"Darling, I know you love me because you just told me so yourself, and what I'm asking you here, what I'm really asking you has to do with what people in love, such as we are, might sometimes ask the other loved one to do. Namely, please, just this once, help me out and don't tell a single soul."

"But why? Why is what I'm asking you."

"Sometimes, my sugar cube, two people love each other so much that they don't have to ask silly little questions like *why?* Because really, if you really want to know the truth, the why isn't all that important in this particular case. I merely find myself at one of those junctures when I feel like I'd really rather not say why, or where, or when. Can you understand, darling? Have I made things a bit clearer for you?"

"Well, I suppose I understand, but really I don't. I mean I understand what you mean, but I don't understand why you're doing it in the first place," she said.

"That's just great. So we have a deal then? Great. I knew I

could count on you. I just knew that of all the people left on earth, that you I could count on. One other thing, I don't want guests coming over to the house anymore."

# A CALL TO ARMS

I COME TO work, and there on the answering machine I find the message from Darin. The message from Darin confirms all of my worst fears. The message from Darin brings my blood to a boil. It puts all sorts of crazy thoughts into my head, thoughts which no one should think about another living person. The message from Darin means war.

I write down the message in my journal, word for word, rewinding the tape several times so as not to miss a single syllable. My machine has an unlimited message time for callers to talk as long as they like. Darin has chosen to take full advantage of this feature. The message reads as follows:

*Hello, this is Darin. It's ten p.m., and I'm calling this late to make sure you won't be there. Also, I'm at a pay phone, so just in case you are there, screening the calls, you won't try and call me back. Listen, I'm go-*

*ing to get straight to the point. Those messages you left me were really some piece of work. I mean they really say a lot about what a wonderful guy you must be deep down. In fact, they were so wonderful that I saved them. Look, I know you had something to do with the murder. I'm not saying you killed her, or anything like that, but you do know something. My advice to you is simple. Seek help, and go to the police with what you know. Now I'm going to tell you a few things about the woman who was killed. Her name was Luciana Mattere and she lived here for only four months before her death. She grew up in an orphanage outside of Florence, then moved to Rome to become a model. I met her inside the camera that day that you yourself now acknowledge as having happened. We talked a great deal, much to your dismay, about everything, art, music, the camera obscura, our lives. We arranged to meet later that night to continue our discussion. If you haven't turned off the message by now let me tell you that by then I had already fallen in love with the woman. That night we ended up in bed together, a memory I won't ever surrender. The ensuing weeks were filled with more of the same, long walks, endless conversation, and romance. I know you probably don't believe any of this. Anyway, that final evening, when you saw both of us on the cliffs, I proposed marriage to her. She accepted. Do you believe me when I tell you she accepted? I don't expect so. I can understand how you felt about her, how you wanted her, in fact it was because of this that we never went to the camera together, out of respect for your feelings, but you, you went too far. How do I know you wanted her? Because once I peeked in your journal when you were in the bathroom. You know what I saw, don't you? That was only a week before the murder. The journal is yours, private, I'm not interested in your sexual fantasies, but if you have anything in there regarding her death you'd better come out with it. It's quite evident to me that you do know something. Personally I've decided to go to the police and tell them everything, about you, and about me. After the murder I had to get away, out to the country to clear my head. I know I should have gone to the police right then and there and if I could do it all over again I would, but I was too screwed up inside. I couldn't see straight, not that you care one way or the other about any of it. Most importantly, I have an alibi for the night of the killing, and hope you do as well. I'll wait twenty-four hours before I go to them, which will give you enough time to think over what I've said. That's really all I have to say to you. Good-bye.*

Alibi? Alibi? Alibi! Darin, an innocent man needs no alibi. Think, for twenty-four hours, think. Read my journal! Is there a greater crime than invading another person's private world? Why have you waited until now to go to the police? Who is in hot water, Darin? Asked her to marry you? No doubt you lied when you said she said yes. No doubt in my mind. This really, I mean, this really takes the fucking cake if ever anything did. Twenty-four hours. You killed her, didn't you? When she refused your hand in marriage. When she laughed, looked at you and laughed when you asked, because she had never heard anything so preposterous in all of her life. Laughed in your face, Darin!

It's then that I start getting nervous. Where is Darin? I mean, the man's a possible murderer. He could be watching me right now. I move away from the ticket booth window, lock the door and take the journal and the answering machine inside the chamber. I write every word down.

After a while I begin to relax as the image on the screen glides along in its mezmerising circle. The windmills in the park, then the beach. You fool, Darin, idiot, imbecile. Leave me alone was what I told you, just leave me alone. The reflection of the sun glimmers on the sea as the periscope passes the point where the waves gently break.

You had me duped, that's for sure. Who would have thought you had it in you, such a seemingly harmless kid. The rocks come into view, some birds hover in a holding pattern, riding currents of wind, some have landed.

Why go after me? You'd run for your life if you had any smarts, out of the country. The cliffs are coming up next. Wait! A wave of paranoia overcomes me. Stop the periscope before they come into view! I yank down the lever and halt the image of the rocks, the birds and the sea, only inches away from where the cliffs begin.

He'll be there. I know it, in the spot where he killed her, waiting, waiting for the periscope so that he can stare me down. Darin! I yell and move away from the screen, trembling, backing up until I hit the wall.

Five minutes go by, and still I'm shaking. Frozen in place like the birds hovering on the screen. What if he's not there? Maybe I'm wrong. I could be wrong, and if I am then I'm standing here for nothing. Convince yourself that he's not there, I think. What are you going on anyway? A feeling? Intuition?

Christ, get a hold of yourself. Pull the lever and find out one way or another.

Five more minutes, and finally frustration begins to set in. Then anger. You will not get the better of me, Darin! I lean forward and push the lever into position. The periscope silently turns to the right, exposing barren cliffs. I can feel my pulse in my hands, my feet, my temples. No Darin. It's a wonder I didn't faint at that moment.

There will come a day, Darin, when you'll wish you'd never disturbed my privacy, when you'll wish you'd never set foot in the camera obscura.

# DISASTER

CORNELIUS DREBBLE WENT directly to Vermeer's apartment. The charade had lasted long enough. Love conquered all fear. Love held his resolve, his fate. He knocked loudly on the door, he screamed Vermeer's name, he pounded again, but still no answer. In a fit of desperation he took two steps back and hurled his body at the door, bursting it open, badly bruising his shoulder.

Vermeer waited silently upstairs in the darkened chamber that had once been his living room. His wife had gone off to her sister's house. Through the camera obscura Vermeer had seen Drebble coming from across the river. It was the opportunity he had waited for.

What choice did Vermeer have? No choice. Cornelius Drebble must not tell a single soul about the camera obscura, that Vermeer used it to paint his masterpieces. Insurance, real insurance, not just a handshake or a promise, but a way to make sure the word wouldn't get out to the public.

Cornelius Drebble climbed the stairs, out of breath, holding his shoulder. "Hello," he called down the hall. "Vermeer?" But no one answered. He went into the kitchen first, and found Vermeer's journal lying on the table. He flipped it open to the bookmark and read, "I have never seen a sunset more beautiful than today's. Just when the very last tip of the sun fell beneath the horizon the sky lit up with three brilliant flashes of green. They went by so quickly, I'm still not sure whether or not they really happened. With the camera obscura I see things which confuse me every day."

After this entry Drebble wrote a long and detailed confession, the story of his affair with Vermeer's wife. *I love her more than life itself,* he concluded, *and want to marry her. Please agree to meet me so that we might talk like grown men about this most difficult and sensitive problem. Yours, Cornelius Drebble.* He laid the pen down and walked back toward the stairs. Just then he heard a noise in the front room, in the camera obscura. "Who's there?" he called, but again there was no reply. "Vermeer?" Then again, another noise, a scratching.

Inside the chamber, Vermeer took out his old army sword from the closet and hid behind the door. Cornelius Drebble walked toward the room, cautiously, quietly. Vermeer raised the sword high above his head and strengthened his grip. Cornelius Drebble reached for the doorknob.

## CHUANG CHOU, GIVE ME STRENGTH

WHAT CHOICE? WHAT possible choice? I have called Darin's answering machine once every five minutes for the past hour. I have filled his message tape. *From this moment on,* I said in my final address, *you don't exist anymore. You have ceased to exist as a human being on this planet, Darin.*

Drebble's neck is bare, shiny, stretched out perfectly, as he leans his head into the room. So I have no alternative. Isn't it true that I too have but one, singular alternative? Look, if I were Vermeer, the head would already have come off a long time ago. But speaking for Vermeer, as I am now, action doesn't always come as easily as an idea, even with a sharp blade, a bare, fleshy neck, and a darkened room.

What in the hell has happened here? Mona, can you please tell me what in the hell has happened here? Have I so misjudged

Darin? How could I live such a large portion of time deceived with the very idea of that man? Do I really understand the state of things as they stand right now? That Darin will tell the police that I am involved with the murder. That Darin slept with the woman, made love to her right under my nose! That he says he has an alibi, but that he'll give me twenty-four hours before going to the police. Why? Why twenty-four hours? To turn myself in? A favor, I suppose.

What evidence? What possible evidence? The journal, yes, but what if there never was a journal, or it couldn't be produced in the courtroom? Nobody saw me that night. They don't know when I left the camera. The messages I left on Darin's machine? What could I have said? I yelled, so what, a lot of people yell. I said something about the police. Don't go to the police, or it doesn't make any sense to go to the police. Could you really take a simple little sentence like that and twist it into murder? Because when he starts going on about the journal, about how I had some strange fantasy world in which I worshipped her, well then what evidence, what journal? And when the prosecution finds no journal, what have they got? They've got zero.

Swipe, chop, snap, thud. The mess, the ungodly mess of it. Drebble's body leaking blood all over, his head wobbling in a semicircle on the floor. Vermeer, what have you done? Look what a terrible thing you have just done. What to do? What to do now?

Life without the journal won't be easy. All of my research. I will miss it more than I can possibly envision. How shall I dispose of the notebooks? Burn them, the obvious, almost inevitable choice. But first, one final story, or a trip out to the cliffs? What would I see at this point? What could I write?

Perhaps I could hide it instead. If only there was some hidden place where the journal would remain safe. Where, say, five or ten years from now I could reclaim it, after all of the commotion had died down. Of course such a place exists. Take the head for instance, never found. Did I mention that the head was never recovered?

Vermeer, think, think and act. You've got a dead body on your hands, you've got the murder weapon in them. Move man! Move! Your wife will arrive home very shortly. Very, very soon your wife will arrive home. Not that she'll see anything. Your wife is blind, Vermeer. But her sister will see, because her sister has to accompany her home. And if she comes upstairs for a cup of coffee, which she does from time to time, she's going to notice an odd smell, and will no doubt see the pool of blood now creeping its way into the hall. All very bad for you, because you know who your wife's sister's husband is, don't you? Yes, you do, the chief of police. Take the head, take the body, take the sword and go hide them for God sakes! Then bring the mop from the kitchen. Time is short!

Oh yes, oh yes, oh yes, don't I know just the spot? Don't I already have the perfect place in mind? I do, I do. Beyond the parking lot, yes? A good two hundred yards from the scene of the crime. I've got to hand it to myself this time. The perfect place. What I did was dig a hole, a hole underneath a rock, and in the hole I put a wooden box. I built the box myself, and put a lock on the lid for safe keeping. Surely the journal will fit in the box. Surely, ample space remains inside of the wooden box. Space I kept available for future use.

So he takes a shovel and digs. All of this in broad daylight, can you imagine? A body, a head, a sword, and him there digging, but you know what? Not one single soul even saw him. He dug and dug, until finally he had himself a very large hole. First he dragged the body over to it, then the head, and then the sword. Finally, he sprinkled a large bag of coffee over the whole mess, yes coffee, because he read somewhere that coffee covered up the smell of practically everything, that dogs could never get past the smell of it even when the body started to decay. When he had finished covering up the hole he went upstairs to mop up the blood. Into the kitchen for a bucket and some soap, but what's this? What do we have here? Vermeer's journal lying open on the kitchen table, and what a curious scrawl fills the page! Vermeer sits and begins deciphering the pages of confession, all the while his emotions steadily growing, delight mixed with feverish rage. Truly Drebble had received his just fate. Could there be a surer sign than his own written testimony? Reading it filled Vermeer with a sense that justice had prevailed, and he wished he could kill Drebble all over again. But what about his wife? His wife, the woman he adored, who never once caused the slightest doubt to cross his mind regarding her loyalty, her purity. What should become of her?

Furiously, he ripped out the pages from his journal and looked around for a match to burn them with. He knocked over glasses, threw plates, kicked over the kitchen table and then did the same to the bedroom, all the while cursing the day he met his wife.

In the living room, the dark chamber, he attempted to compose his thoughts. He closed the door and sat in a chair in front of the camera obscura. His breathing slowed down, he crossed his legs, and stared at the screen on the wall for what seemed like an hour. He could see a reflection of the setting sun in a window opposite his house, it made its way slowly towards the horizon. Vermeer saw the bottom tip melt into the west end of the river. "What's done is done," he said to himself. "There's no need for hasty action."

The sun sank below the watery horizon, and in the window Vermeer saw another inexplicable flash of green light. He searched the screen for an answer and suddenly noticed his wife and her sister sitting on a park bench just on the other side of the river. It seemed as if the sister had also seen the flash of green light and was trying to explain it to Vermeer's wife.

Vermeer jumped up, ran into the kitchen and began mopping and rearranging the whole house with the same vigor he had used to wreck it. He hid the journal pages behind the camera screen, prepared an alibi as to the broken dishes. "I couldn't stand to see us eat off of such rotten dishes, such ugly, filthy, rotten dishes for another second. Honey, what we deserve is a new set of china." The door opened downstairs just as he had mopped up the last puddle in the hallway. "Darling?" he called. "Is that you?"

Good-bye to the journal. Good-bye for the time being. Before leaving the camera I shall focus the periscope on the cliffs. When I have buried the box I shall stroll out to the cliffs. When I am standing at the cliffs watching the sunset I will look for the green flash, and I'll try and imagine my own image on the camera's radiant screen. Without the journal these fleeting moments will disappear, untouched by history. But no time for regrets. Onward, to the task at hand. Woman from Florence, Luciana Mattere, please forgive me.

You got away with it, didn't you Vermeer, you crafty devil! At this time I should like to offer up my belated congratulations, not that there isn't still unfinished business out there concerning your wife, but I'm sure that you'll work something out. Just as I will attend to that little problem named Darin. Really it's just a question of when and where. Yes, there's definitely plenty of room in the box.

Put the pen down. Put it down for the time being. The official story, because the police will want a good one, must read as follows: *A man who owned his own business, a good business, where the tourists could enjoy a beautiful view of a beautiful spot in nature. A man who minded his own business, kept to himself, but was always friendly to his customers. Moreover, the man felt content with a life by the sea. Never did he feel the need to write down his thoughts, for his thoughts were at peace. What would the man possibly write? What life could he possibly envision as more complete and fulfilling than the one that he had chosen? Man and the sea.* The story of the man now reads without a hitch.

The sound-track tape, I almost forgot. Destroy it too. Destroy all evidence of distraction from the pure and noble life of the simple man and the camera obscura, mere tool for witnessing the glory of the world. No life exists within the camera itself, rather the device functions merely as a frame for the living world. On a new tape I will explain the basic mechanical procedures and the camera's scientific uses by the great astronomer Johann Kepler.

Cut the ties with art altogether. Down with the Mona Lisa. There's no proof, I will say, that the Chinese invented it, or that any of them used it, Leonardo, Vermeer. No doubt that's what I'll tell them. Not that I really know that much about it one way or the other.

And with the transformation all secrets will be kept safe, and the questioning will cease. Now, put the pen down. Put it down with the knowledge that it will wait, in a darkened chamber with this journal and a sword and a head and some coffee, for the stories of the past to re-emerge some other day.